The Return of Count Electric & Other Stories

by

WILLIAM BROWNING SPENCER

The Permanent Press
SAG HARBOR, NEW YORK 11963

Library of Congress Cataloging-in-Publication Data

Spencer, William Browning, 1946–
    The Return of Count Electric, and Other Stories / by William Browning Spencer.
      p. cm.
    ISBN 1-877946-27-3 : $21.95
    1. Fantastic fiction, American. I. Title.
PS3569.P458B47   1993
813'.54—dc20
                                                  92-34299
                                                    CIP

Manufactured in the United States of America

THE PERMANENT PRESS
Noyac Road
Sag Harbor, NY 11963

This book is dedicated to
my parents

Table of Contents

Introduction   7

The Wedding Photographer In Crisis   13

Haunted by the Horror King   25

The Entomologists At Obala   35

The Return of Count Electric   59

Graven Images   75

Pep Talk   83

Looking Out For Eleanor   91

Snow   157

A Child's Christmas In Florida   175

Best Man   183

Daughter Doom   193

Introduction

In the spring of 1990, my first novel, *Maybe I'll Call Anna*, was published. Shortly after its publication, I moved to Austin, Texas, got a job working the night shift at the local newspaper, and set about writing another novel. Then I fell in with a crowd of short story writers. . . .

The short story has much to recommend it to the writer, and its greatest virtue, its most seductive quality is, of course, its length. A short story can be written quickly. It can then be read to an audience. The writing of novels is, by comparison, a long, lonely trek through hostile country.

I wrote my first short story—a sort of homage to M.R. James—during a bout with the flu. I might have resisted the short story, had I been in perfect health. Who knows? I wrote the story while lying in bed and sent it off to an editor at *Weird Tales* who said he liked it and would buy it were it not that his magazine had a two-year inventory of material.

I took this letter as a positive sign, and I began to produce short stories and to send them to those few paying magazines that publish fiction. The stories were returned.

Every writer receives rejection slips. These rejections are to be expected and may even be helpful to him, leading naturally to the development of a reclusive, skeptical nature and allowing the writer to remain alone in a room for long periods of time without pining for the company of others.

But there was something about these magazine rejections. . . . I had, after all, had some experience with rejection while writing longer works of fiction, and the tone here was different. For example: Several months after sending a short story to *The Boston Review*, I received a form rejection letter ("it does not suit our needs at this time" et cetera) upon which some anonymous employee had scrawled the following: "P.S. Your submission had a good second and last paragraph."

I tried to envision the sort of writer who would be heartened by such a statement. Was it possible that there existed a writer so craven, so devoid of self-worth, so riddled with doubt, that he would see this smug pronouncement as something positive? I did not understand, then, how thoroughly cowed and demoralized the writer of short fiction can become as he encounters a world in which supply vastly outweighs demand. Magazines that pay nothing for a story routinely receive five hundred stories a month and take four months to reply.

"Why don't these magazines pay money?" the new writer asks. The editors of these magazines answer, with irrefutable logic and some heat: "We don't pay money because we don't make money." In other words, there isn't . . . well . . . an audience. Okay, the new short story writer responds, if no one is listening, then I suppose I'm willing to talk for free.

But why isn't anyone listening? Did the reading public have, in fact, some good reason for avoiding these stories?

I began reading short stories for the first time in years. It seemed to me that short fiction had changed since those earlier days when I had read it voraciously. These stories seemed more opaque, less . . . well, less *fun*.

Fun? Not much of a critical assessment, and I might have remained in the dark, were it not for a local weekly entertainment newspaper, which sponsored a short story contest. The winners were instructive. All five winners produced excellent writing. These were stories that judges would immediately recognize as examples of fine writing. The metaphors were elegant and of the sort that only occur to writers. Four of the five stories were written in the present tense. The stories tended to be about childhood and adolescence and centered around some telling metaphor. For instance, one of the stories ended with the narrator watching a child stand on a pier and throw shells into the water. The pier (we are told in the last line) "looks collapsible and strong at the same time." Keep in mind that we have not encountered this child before. The child is there at the end of the story, so that the point about life can be made.

If these stories are representative (and I think they probably are) of the direction short stories are taking, then the actual telling of stories has ceased to be of interest to the practitioners of this art form. Only one of these five stories actually offered a story that could be *told*, that would be interesting in its bare, fireside recitation. The present tense (which can leach the drama from any scene) was a clue here. People appeared to move as though underwater ("She walks to the door. She opens the door. She sees the newspaper lying on the grass").

As a writer, I have to assume that someone is listening. To whom is the modern short story being addressed? I believe, sadly, that it is being addressed to other writers, that it is wrought in the laboratory of the creative writing class and is uncomfortable in the larger world. The short story has become something to admire rather than love.

Raymond Carver wrote stories of blue collar workers who encountered some event or symbol that summed them up with dreadful clarity. We enlightened readers understood the importance of the event or symbol although the poor lout in the story always missed it. These stories seemed to possess a smirky, intellectual superiority, these stories of used-car salesmen and cab drivers and fast-food workers blundering into academic epiphanies.

Well, it seems to me that the unwashed multitudes had the last laugh. The academics could "get it," but the inner circle grew pretty small. Those who didn't get it simply shrugged, said, "Life is short," and moved on to more entertaining pursuits, including the novels of folks like Larry McMurtry, Pat Conroy, John Irving and Stephen King who still believed, like Homer, that you had to be talking to some purpose, that there had to, finally, be a tale to unfold.

Obviously, there is a place for those short stories whose aims and methods are more closely allied to poetry. What threatens the well-being of the short story, what may indeed lead to its ultimate demise except as a kind of arcane craft, is the dominance of short fiction as extended metaphor, fine writing for the sake of fine writing, critical disparagement of plot, and a general disregard for the reader's right to some narrative movement. When the heroine of a short story wraps a baloney sandwich in cellophane before falling asleep on the sofa, the reader has the legitimate right to demand why two thousand words are exhausted for that purpose. It does not seem enough to reply that never in the history of the short story has the wrapping of a baloney sandwich been described with such elegance, with such an awareness of the mundane, with such a keen ear for the crackle of cellophane and with such sardonic wit.

Well, I've digressed some myself—as though you had all day. Enclosed are stories, some of which can, I suppose, be taken to task for possessing the very qualities I've inveighed against. I've done my best to tell compelling stories. It's up to

10

you to decide whether I've done that or not. I've tried to please myself, which is all, really, any writer who is also a reader can do.

I wish to thank Marty and Judy Shepard for publishing these stories, for their enthusiasm and support—and for the suggestion that I launch this collection with an intro.

The Wedding Photographer In Crisis

When Patricia left, I got rid of everything and moved into an apartment. By everything, I mean everything. I bought new clothes, a new TV, new furniture. Even my toothbrush was new. I believe in making a clean break with the past.

The past can hide in anything. A sofa you have had for ten years can be infested with old memories. Don't try to salvage it. Sell it. Give it to the Salvation Army. Burn it. A china lamp that you have owned for seven years will begin to look like a disapproving in-law. Take that lamp to a party and plug it in. Don't take it with you when you leave.

And photographs. Do I want to see Patricia and me at Atlantic City biting down on opposite ends of a hot dog or would I rather live out my life with a piece of dental floss stuck between my teeth? Tear up photographs and burn them as first measures in destroying them. That's my advice. I really hate photographs, although I am, by trade, a photographer.

That's me: *Don's Quality Photo.* I'm Don—a big guy with a mustache that is maybe getting a little out of hand and kind, watery blue eyes. You might guess, looking at me, that I had suffered some tragedy. You would be right. My twin brother Duane, the companion of my youth, was hit and killed by a bakery truck careening down an icy road when we were twelve. To this day I will not touch pastries,

13

and there is a part of me that is missing. I often forget where I am or what enterprise requires my immediate attention.

In my business, I take a lot of pictures of children, and I am good with them. My secret is that I think of them as crazy people, and I don't expect much. Patricia—who used to help in the studio—preferred to think of children as rudimentary adults who could be reasoned with in an adult fashion. This doomed approach often made her vicious and frustrated, and while I will not lay the blame for our divorce on this one aspect of our relationship, it certainly contributed to our downfall as a couple. Attitude is everything in a marriage.

I also take a lot of photos of weddings. I prefer outdoor ones, where I can use the available light. Indoors, I often have to resort to electronic flash, and the resulting photos aren't always all I would wish them to be. Electronic flash is a cruel reporter, and it can take the loveliest bride and make her look like she is made out of cheap vinyl. White bridal gowns are turned into eye-searing explosions of light, and the surrounding celebrants smile from the depths of a sort of brown soup that the flash has refused to penetrate. The stop-action nature of flash suggests that its subjects have been surprised in the midst of clandestine activities, like leaving a motel room after a rendezvous with an evangelist, and a common expression in these photos is a smile so false that any man sporting such a smile in, say, a public restroom, would immediately be arrested by the first undercover cop encountering him. In these photos, the eyes of participants often glow redly.

But every profession has its downside, and I generally enjoy my work. I am not troubled by other people's photos. It is true that I am supplying folks with the documentation that may one day rise up to make them miserable, but I try not to think about that. Besides, I am optimistic when it comes to other folks. I believe in happy endings. I believe there are a lot of people out there who will lead good, full lives and will find, in old photos, nothing but fond memories.

When I go to weddings, I find that I always get sentimental. I have heard "The Wedding Song" I don't know how many times, and it always chokes me up. I am oddly touched by so many people in tuxedos and fancy dresses. How, I reason, can life be meaningless if people are willing to dress so elaborately for it? A mere photographer, trying to be as unobtrusive as a fat man with a camera can be, I sometimes find myself hugging total strangers, lifting elderly women right off their feet in a fit of congratulatory high-spirits, kissing small pink-and-white girls, slapping the backs of nervous, pale young men.

So I was looking forward to the ceremony, and I got there early. St. Vincent's, a big church with a number of needle-sharp spires and lots of stained-glass martyrs, presided over five acres of green hills. The ceremony was to be held outside, by the side of a small pond. It was mid-October, a brisk, Northern Virginia morning, and the sun was bright and only occasionally obscured by huge, regal cumulus clouds.

The wedding was to take place at eleven, but I had told everyone to be dressed and ready by nine so I could take those "before" pictures so necessary to any wedding photo album. What album would be complete without the gag picture of the best man dragging the groom back into the room or the photo of the bride, surrounded by anxious relatives, hyperventilating into a paper bag?

I had taken two dozen photos of the bride, a small, delicate blonde girl as high-strung as a penthouse poodle and trapped in a vast bridal gown. The image of a tiny child sinking into an immense wedding cake lodged in my mind and could not be dislodged. After that photo session, I had documented various permutations of parents and friends and children and I was snapping some photos of the bridesmaid, a buxom, red-headed girl of perhaps twenty-five. She was a cheerful girl with a round face, bright blue eyes, and a wide, wanton mouth.

Sensing that in this girl I had found a good sport, I had escorted her to a small auxiliary chapel on the grounds and prevailed upon her to display her excellent breasts for my camera.

"I don't know," she said, expressing token resistance.

"I'm a professional," I assured her.

I might have persuaded her to offer up other charms to the camera, but I remembered that I had yet to photograph the groom, and so I had to cut short the session. I did obtain her telephone number.

Returning to the church, I learned that the groom had not yet arrived. His bride-to-be was worried. Her mother, a large, silver haired woman wearing a substantial investment in cosmetics, consoled her. "I'm sure he'll be here any minute," she said, with such an utter lack of conviction that I found myself becoming alarmed. They had called the groom's house but the phone had gone unanswered.

Patricia always told me that I am too quick to take on the troubles of others. "They don't want your help. They are not your responsibility." She was right, of course. But the father of the bride was absent—dead, as a matter of fact—and the bride's mother was tottering on high heels and smelling strongly of gin. Debbie (the bride) seemed to be sinking into her glorious gown without one rescuer, one champion, in sight.

And when I learned that the groom, John Teller by name, lived less than a mile from St. Vincent's, I didn't see any reason why I couldn't, myself, swing by and see what the delay was all about.

The address proved to be a two-story wooden house in a sea of tall grass. No one answered when I knocked on the door. I turned the knob and the door opened.

"Hello?" I shouted.

I walked into a dark living room. A young man slept on the sofa in his underwear, and another young man slept on the floor. The guy on the floor lay on his back, fully dressed, with his arms flung out as though crucified.

"John Teller?"

The kid opened his eyes and sat up. "Who are you?" he asked. He wore black: black tennis shoes, black jeans, black sweatshirt.

"Don Robeson," I told him. "I am photographing Mr. Teller's wedding," I explained, "so it is imperative that I locate him."

The kid lay back down and put an arm over his eyes. "Shit," he said. "I think it is off. I mean, we had this bachelor party last night, and John had this insight . . . I mean, he understood suddenly that he was not a marrying kind of person, that being married didn't integrate with his personality, wasn't an identity he could comfortably own, you know?"

I asked where the insightful Mr. Teller could be found and was directed up a flight of stairs.

"That's right," Teller told me. "Debbie is a great girl, and my decision has nothing to do with her. I just can't marry her after all." Teller was unshaven, red-eyed, with a fuzzy cloud of light brown hair.

I looked at my watch. It was 10:15. "Too late," I said.

Teller mumbled something and pulled the covers up over his head.

I extracted him from the bed and thumped him against the wall to shake the sleep out of him.

"What the fuck!" he screamed. I do not like to manhandle skinny young men in boxer shorts. I was wearing a brown suit which was off the rack and showing its age, but a man in a suit always has a certain moral advantage over a man in his underwear, and I didn't want to unfairly press that advantage. I urged Teller to don the tuxedo that was still draped across a chair where he had placed it before deciding that he was not suited for marriage. By way of incentive, I massaged his throat.

"Aaaaak," Teller said, which I interpreted as a desire to get dressed. I let go, and he bolted for the bedroom door. I am, however, quicker than my appearance would suggest. I retrieved Teller, dragged him to the window, opened the window, and, retaining a firm grip on his ankles, dangled the young man in the chill October air. I felt that the autumn air and the blood rushing to his head would restore clarity to his thinking and destroy at least a few of the cobwebs that late hours and overindulgence had created. I was right in this, and he was able to understand and appreciate the nature of my request. Back in the room, he dressed hurriedly.

"You'll want to shave," I said.

"No I won't," he said.

I escorted him to the bathroom and helped him shave. Early in the process, Teller asserted his independence, and I ceased to offer assistance. He did a passable job, although a few bits of toilet paper had to be applied to staunch the bleeding of several nicks.

I hitched my camera bag over my shoulder as we marched downstairs. "Don't try anything," I said. Thanks to the shared experience of television, Teller knew exactly what this meant, and he didn't try anything. We marched past his fellow celebrants, who were sleeping soundly.

"Rings!" I shouted. "We almost forgot the rings!" The best man—in black and unconscious on the floor—had the rings in his pockets. I shook them out, and we were on our way again.

"You can drive," I said, giving Teller the keys to my truck. I sat in the passenger seat and fished through my camera bag.

"I don't know how you think you can make me go through with this, mister. And what is it to you anyway?"

"I'm the photographer," I told him. "How am I supposed to get the pictures if the wedding doesn't occur?"

"I don't think that you appreciate what's going on here. You're talking about my life, the rest of my goddam life."

I had found what I was looking for, a silver thirty-eight pistol, as bright and beautiful as any jewel. I pulled it out and, pointing it at Teller, I shouted: "I WILL FUCKING BLOW YOUR HEAD OFF IF YOU DON'T MARRY DEBBIE! GOT THAT?"

I startled him, I guess, because he drove the pickup off the road and onto the sidewalk. He was resilient however, and wrestled the truck back onto the road.

He was whispering under his breath, saying "Jesus," I think.

"I'm sorry," I said. "I didn't mean to alarm you. But I feel strongly about this. The question, I suppose is: 'Does a wedding exist so that it can be photographed, or are the photographs a mere by-product of the wedding?' Which comes first, the chicken or the egg? I'm no philosopher, but I *am* a photographer, so you can guess how I feel about it."

"You are crazy," Teller said.

As we drove along, I studied my young companion. He had combed his hair and looked considerably better than when I had first encountered him. I put the gun down. It was not loaded and I had never fired it. I had received it as partial payment for a wedding that spring, and I had been intending to sell it. Maybe I would hang onto it after all. I lifted my camera, and snapped Teller's profile as we flew toward the church and his destiny. One day, perhaps, he would encounter this photo, laugh, draw a curly-headed grandson closer and say, "Those little white flecks are toilet paper. Yes! I cut myself shaving that morning. I was a wreck that day, let me tell you, so nervous . . ."

"We'll have to find another best man," I said.

Teller said nothing. We turned into the church's driveway. I looked at my watch.

"Fifteen minutes to spare," I said.

We recruited one of the ushers for best man honors, gave him the rings and some hurried instructions.

I needed to get moving in order to document the bride and groom's approach. "See you at the altar," I said, leaning forward and clutching young Teller's arm. I gave it a good squeeze to convey the depth of my sincerity, and then I was off, running down the hill toward the pond, a fat man pursuing his vocation, approaching a colorful crowd fidgeting upon folding chairs. The minister—Episcopalian, I believe—stood at the edge of the pond with a Bible pressed comfortably against his chest.

The ceremony went smoothly, although, to my way of thinking, it could have been shorter. The minister made a long speech about the solemnity and sanctity of marriage in these troubled times, and it was a speech that ranged over a variety of topics, including the destruction of the ozone layer.

"Okay, okay," I muttered as I snapped photographs. "Let's get this show on the road."

I got all the obligatory shots: the kiss, the bouquet in the air, the always-awkward garter bit, the cutting of the cake. The obligatory stray dog drifted in and ran off with a little girl's hat. A rock band whose youngest member must have been fifty played old Beatles' songs loudly and ineptly.

I looked at the young couple. Teller had his arm around Debbie's waist. The glowing bride, although still suggesting a child being swallowed by a monstrous cake, seemed to have accepted her fate. She no longer looked terrified, and as I watched, it was clear that she was instructing her new husband regarding some matter of etiquette.

Young Teller was beaming, awash on the great wave of adulation and good will that buoys up all young couples on their wedding day. No doubt this emotion was transient, and the young couple might fight before the day was over, might slam doors in some motel room, might hold each other's faults up to a cold light, might cry and rage.

As I drove away, I realized that I myself was emotionally drained—and I was only the photographer.

I didn't want to drive home. I wasn't up to facing my apartment, so I drove to a bar, had a few drinks, and gave Patricia a call from the pay phone near the restrooms.

She answered the phone on the second ring. "Hey, how you doing?" I asked.

Patricia is not good on phones. I've seen her from the other side, and it is clear that she hates talking on the phone. The minute she answers, she wants to hang up. She'll pace up and down with the receiver lodged between shoulder and ear while she lights a cigarette, one eye closed. She'll be moving fast, from the kitchen to the living room, going the length of the cord like a hooked fish. "Yeah, yeah, yeah," she'll say, as though she has heard everything the caller has to say before—and often. She's that way with everyone, so I don't take it personally.

"I just thought I'd see what was up," I said. "I'm thinking of coming by this weekend."

She said she didn't think that would be a good idea; she had plans.

"Maybe next week then," I said. "I'll give you a call before then."

"Every day," she said.

"What's that?"

"Don, you call every day," she said.

"That often, huh?"

"Yeah," she said. Little choppy sentences are one technique people use to terminate conversations. The theory, I guess, is that if you don't offer anything for the conversation to feed on it will eventually die, starve.

I always find it sort of a challenge to see how long I can keep Patricia on the phone, though.

I logged maybe fifteen minutes before she said she heard someone at the door.

I went back to the bar and drank a few more beers. I lost track of time and didn't get home until real late, hauled the cameras and lenses and crap up the three flights, and woke the next day sleeping on the top of the bed. I had wrestled my coat off, and my tie was on the floor, but I still had my shoes on. That's always a bad sign—sleeping in your shoes— and I resolved to cut down on the drinking.

I sat on the side of the bed and looked at the photo of Patricia on the wall. Okay, I've still got one photo. And okay, okay, it is big. I mean, it's a poster I had made: 3 feet by 4 feet. I snapped it when we were down at Nags Head, and it isn't great art or anything. It's contrasty, and her eyes are half-closed with the sun in her face, and you can see the waves behind her and it is grainy and kind of embarrassing— me being a photographer and all I should have something a little more artful on my wall—but she has this dazzle of smile and her hair is still wet from the ocean and unraveling down the left side of her face like a handful of bright yellow ribbons.

And I was telling the truth about hating the past and loathing all the accusations and regrets that old photos fill up with.

But this photo is different. I can see myself telling my grandson, "That's Grandma at the beach."

It's a rare photo, somehow hopeful, without a bit of sorrow or blighted hope in it. Hell, I might have taken it just yesterday.

Haunted By The Horror King

During the day it is okay, but at night I am sleeping in my room, and suddenly I snap awake. I know what has awakened me, but I have to slow my breathing and wait before I hear it again. At first I hear nothing but the snores of my roommate, Jack Hodges, a large, gloomy black man who told me—my first day here—not to worry; he wasn't violent as long as he remembered to take his Thorazine.

I keep on listening, with my eyes wide open. Then I hear it. *Click!* It is a dreadful sound, like a switchblade being flicked open in a dark alley. Then: *click, click!* One last pause on a precipice of silence, and then: *click, click, click, click, click, click!*

The noise goes on and on, growing louder, relentless, filling the darkness and making my heart race.

It is the sound of Stephen King's typewriter as he brutally bangs the keys. The sound has traveled across six states, to find me here in this mental health facility in Northern Virginia. I lie in bed, helpless, listening to the words being hammered out and falling—*click, click, click*—like cold rain on my heart.

When Elaine comes to visit, she tries to disabuse me of this notion. "Stephen King doesn't even write on a typewriter," she says. "He uses a word processor."

"Why should I believe you?" I say. "You're sleeping with him."

Accused, she feigns shock and outrage, and this usually signals the end of our visit.

In group, Danny Wolitzer—who is here because he likes to take off all his clothes while riding buses—says I am crazy.

"Maybe I am, now," I say. "I wasn't always."

I wasn't.

It started in 1978, long before I met and married Elaine. I had written five unpublished novels, and I was just completing my sixth novel while working as a clerk typist for an insurance company. Sarah and I had been living together for a year, and we were, I think, deeply in love.

I gave the finished manuscript to her to read. She was the person whose opinion mattered most to me, and I was certain she would love this novel. It was the best thing I had ever written, a dark and haunting foray into the mind of an aging high school English teacher.

Knowing Sarah's reaction would be positive, I was still jittery and had to leave the apartment to avoid popping in on her every five minutes to ask how it was going. Adjourning to a nearby bar, I encountered two other writers (an accountant and a used car salesman) and we had a few beers.

When I returned to the apartment, the living room and kitchen were dark. There was a light coming from the bedroom, however, and I tiptoed in, thinking to observe the play of emotions on my beloved's face as she read my novel. Perhaps I would find her just as she read that heartrending section where my hero is forced to retire.

My darling lay propped up in bed, three pillows behind her, and the expression on her face was, indeed, enraptured—

everything an author could hope for, really. But she was not reading my manuscript; she was reading a hardcover book.

"Sarah," I said, bursting into the room.

She was caught and she knew it. "Oh," she said, laying the book down (but even then—dear God what inconstancy have you wrought in women!—she held her place with an index finger). "I didn't hear you come in."

"I guess not," I said, and I leaned over and snatched the book from her.

It was a fat, shiny book printed by Doubleday—a publisher whose interest I coveted. Need I say it? The book was *The Stand*; its author Stephen King.

Sarah had purchased the book that morning, begun reading it during her lunch break, and been unable to put it down. With the best intentions in the world, she had begun to read my manuscript, but then—just as murderers come out of a daze with the bloody knife clenched tightly and the bodies strewn about—she unaccountably found herself immersed in *The Stand*.

I suggested—rather stiffly—that she finish *The Stand* so that she could give my manuscript her undivided attention, and with unseemly alacrity, Sarah accepted this proposal.

She dispatched *The Stand* in no time at all and then read my manuscript, declaring it a brilliant, poetic achievement. But she was too late with her praise. Faith had been broken, and I suspected that her enthusiasm was all a sham. I knew where her true affections lay. One night I surprised her at the kitchen table, writing a letter. She quickly folded it and left the room. I looked at the blank tablet she had been writing on. The indentations of her ballpoint pen revealed just enough to confirm what I already suspected. She had been writing a fan letter. To whom? Guess.

Our lives went on. My manuscript was returned by innumerable New York publishers and agents. "This is a good mid-list book," one agent wrote, "but unfortunately, there is no mid-list anymore. What we want is a blockbuster, I'm afraid. This book just doesn't pack the wallop contemporary audiences require. The psychological insights are excellent, but you might think of beefing them up with some popular elements—horror, perhaps. You might take a look at *The Shining* by Stephen King."

I quit the insurance company. They were beginning to make too many demands. I found employment as a dishwasher in an all night diner. One morning I came home to hear Sarah talking on the phone about the fire that had started, spontaneously, in the kitchen wastebasket. "Whup!" she said. "Just like that. We were just eating dinner and all of a sudden the wastebasket like exploded, flames right up to the ceiling. No. Absolutely not. We don't smoke or anything and . . ."

I thought nothing of the conversation at the time, assumed she was talking to her friend Janice, and it was much later—years in fact—that I seem to recall a certain evasiveness when I asked her who she was talking to. Did she answer at all? I don't think so.

Some eighteen months later, King published *Firestarter.* I saw no connection at the time. Only later did I piece it together.

A month after the publication of that book, our cat, Winston, was killed out on the highway. I was still working nights, and poor Sarah found the animal's stiff body. I overheard the phone conversation in which she tearfully related the discovery of Winston's body.

"Who was that?" I asked, hurt that she would seek someone else for the full outpouring of her grief.

"Janice," she said, and it never occurred to me that she might be lying.

Later that year, Sarah confessed she was having an affair. "Who?" I demanded.

She refused to say. I tried following her, but she always managed to lose me in a Walden's or a B. Dalton's—she knew my weakness, my inability to leave a bookstore on a moment's notice.

Eight months after this announcement, I found the copy of *Pet Sematary* in the bottom of her dresser, and suddenly, like a blow to the bridge of the nose, enlightenment came. She was having an affair with Stephen King. He had stolen my wife. He had stolen my dead cat.

She denied it all.

"What about the cat in *Pet Sematary*?" I demanded. I had refused to read the novel—had never read any of them—but a skimming of the opening chapters had revealed a cat and its fate. "There is a dead cat in that book, and it too is killed on the highway."

"Coincidence," Sarah said—a bit quickly, I thought.

"What about the names?" I said.

She did a fair job of looking baffled. "Well, the name of the cat in the book is Church and our cat was named Winston, so, as you say, what about the names?"

I was nodding my head rapidly. "Uh huh, uh huh. And Church is short for Winston Churchill. Winston," I said, with the air of a prosecutor producing a murder weapon. But Sarah was a skilled liar, and she rolled her eyes convincingly and did not crack.

Nonetheless, I knew what I knew. I wrote King a letter telling him to stay away from Sarah. He did not reply. I hadn't expected him to.

I thought of calling his wife. "Tabitha," I would say. "Your husband is unfaithful."

But I didn't do it. Why bother? And Sarah left, moving back to her parents' house in New Orleans.

A year later I met Elaine. She was a lovely, dark-haired woman with gray eyes.

One night, when we were beginning to get serious, I asked her: "Do you like Stephen King?"

"Never read him," she said. "I don't like horror fiction."

I hugged her and let my heart loose. "Go for it, heart," I said to myself.

I married Elaine in a small wedding attended by some of her friends from the department store where she worked and my writer friends.

My writer friends pitched in and got me a pen and pencil set with a silver case. On the case, they had engraved: "May your happiness be unexpurgated." I was touched.

But happiness is always edited by events, and so mine was. At first, we could not have been happier. Elaine was very supportive of my writing. I had been working on a multi-generational novel which I thought had great commercial potential. An agent had expressed interest in the opening chapters. Well, what he had actually said was he would be willing to look at it for a reduced reading fee. I took this as a hopeful sign, and so did Elaine.

You know what is coming, of course. I came home from work for lunch—I had taken a job as a telephone solicitor and my hours were flexible. Elaine was cozily—and the word "brazenly" comes to mind—settled in an armchair and—yes—she was reading Stephen King. The book was *The Tommyknockers*.

"Elaine," I said, trying to control my voice. "I thought you didn't read horror fiction?"

And my beloved replied, oblivious to my pain, "I don't. A friend said this one was science fiction. I'm crazy about science fiction. And you know, this isn't half bad."

I said nothing and went into the study to work on the final

30

draft of my manuscript, tentatively entitled *Sinew* or perhaps *Sinews*. It was almost finished and when, in fact, I finished it the following week, I asked Elaine if she would like to read it. My wife said that she certainly would after she finished *Cujo*, a King novel about a rabid dog. She had decided to go back and read all his books, beginning with *Carrie*. She was now at *Cujo*.

"I thought . . ." I began, but she had already immersed herself in the book and what did it matter what I thought? I sent my novel off to the agent, and he wrote back to say that it was a large book and would require some time to read and, time being money, would cost more than he had initially stated.

I sent him the extra money and waited. Several months passed and I called his office. After some equivocating, a secretary admitted that he worked there, but she said he was on vacation. I practiced patience. Three months later he responded. The letter seemed inordinately short considering the money. It read: "A near-miss here. The characterization is good, but the pace flags. You might look at Stephen King's *Firestarter* to get a feel for pacing. As it stands, I'm afraid it lacks the focus to penetrate today's competitive market. Till next time. Best."

It was somewhere around this time that I began to hear Stephen King's typewriter, clacking away at three in the morning, carried on a chill ghost wind all the way from Maine. I identified it easily enough.

In the grocery store lines his face stared at me from *People* magazine. Newspapers and television also carried his image. I tried to write another novel, but my thoughts would be scattered by the din of his typewriter, and my resolve would be crushed by the force of his hideous industry.

My telephone soliciting job suffered. I found myself asking

total strangers: "Do you read Stephen King?" and when they answered in the affirmative, I would hang up without even attempting a magazine sale.

And then Elaine began having an affair with him. I know. I know. It seems outrageous, doesn't it? But on the title page of her copy of *Misery* was written: "To Elaine—You are my premier hot mamma, Big Steve."

"What's this?" I had demanded of Elaine.

"Steve Clarendon in Appliances gave me the book. He knows I love Stephen King, and he knew it was my birthday, something you forgot," she said. But I know guilt when I see it. I know a woman caught in adultery.

He would call in the night, and I would answer the phone and hear him breathing. He wouldn't talk to me, of course. "Big Steve," I would say. "Leave my wife alone."

I am a strong-willed man and I might have been able to go on, but the republication of *The Stand*, twice as big, kicked me over the edge. I broke the window of the Crown bookstore that contained a display of the obscenely fat book, and, had they not wrestled the gasoline can from me, I would have initiated a roaring bonfire.

I am not, today, repentant—and my doctor, Dr. Abram, knows it.

"And why," he asks, reasonably enough, "would Stephen King, a world famous author who lives in Maine, carry on an affair with your wife, who lives here in Northern Virginia?"

"That is a good question, Dr. Abram." I try to offer positive reinforcement when Dr. Abram asks an intelligent question. "I have, of course, given it considerable thought. I don't know. I have thought perhaps that he is not one man. I have thought that he is the army of the anti-Christ. Perhaps my affliction, that of being cuckolded as a man and ruined as a writer, will begin to befall others. Perhaps you will begin to have many cases like mine, and it will be revealed that Stephen King is a whole army of look-alikes doing Satan's bidding."

"Stephen King as the anti-Christ seems a bit far-fetched," my shrink says.

I shrug my shoulders. "The man's eyebrows are demonic," I say.

Dr. Abram shakes his head sadly.

I have no time to convince Dr. Abram. And what function would it serve? My own soul is lost.

Does that sound melodramatic? Last week, I was in the rec room with my fellow inmates. We were watching some insipid television show about undercover cops in women's clothing. Hugely depressed, I grabbed a paperback and retired to my room. I read half of it before realizing that this tale of vampires was entitled *'Salems Lot* and that its author was . . . you know its author.

It was too late then, and like a man lost to vice, I read recklessly, abandoning myself to the words. The next day I scavenged *Carrie* from a pile of paperback gothics.

I will read whatever of his books I can find in this madhouse. And then—for I have no shame—I will beg my faithless wife to bring me those I still haven't read.

I hear they are coming out with a collection of his blurbs, those quotes that he has strewn across the covers of other authors' books. This may be a rumor. So many rumors surround him.

The Entomologists At Obala

Dear Janey—
I will be giving this letter to a large, evil-looking old man named
Saul who will take it back to Limón. Saul is a devout Christian
and has carved a fish symbol on his forehead and crosses on his
cheeks.
Who knows when this letter will reach you. I am in the rain
forest with Father, having fast-talked him into keeping me with
him for this last leg of the trip. It was close. I was actually at the
airport before tears and a sort of fainting fit convinced him that I
should accompany him.
What's all the fuss, I'd like to know? I've been camping before,
and this is nothing special. It's an easy walk for the most part, since
there isn't much undergrowth in this twilight world. We are still
*three days away from where the wasps (*Philanthus giganticus,*
in case you are taking notes) are supposed to be.
My hair has gone limp, just died. And some fucking bug bit me
on the forehead and I look like I'm sprouting a third eye. I'm glad
Mark isn't here to see me. Father's in a foul mood because a box
of film was either stolen or lost, and my Walkman has been de-
stroyed by—get this!—ants, so I won't be listening to Michael
Bolton in the jungle. Talk about roughing it!
How are you and Tommy getting along? Was it just a steamy
semester's romance or is it lasting through the summer? I was think-

*ing we should rent an apartment off campus next year. I'm sick of
dorms.*

Eve Harper stopped writing. She unsnapped the tent flap
and looked out into the darkness. She could see her father's
tent, illuminated from within, and assumed that he was sort-
ing the insects he had collected during the day. Beyond his
tent, the darkness was immense and filled with noises Eve
couldn't identify—which, she thought, was just as well. And
somewhere out there Saul and the three other dark-skinned,
silent men who had helped lug the equipment into the rain
forest lay sleeping.

Eve felt something skitter across her hand, and she quickly
dropped the tent flap.

She returned to the letter and wrote:

*This is a great adventure but, as usual, Father is doing his
damnedest to make it dull. Every new bug he scoops up comes with
a lecture. I try to look interested, so he won't regret bringing me,
but I'm not riveted, you understand. I know he'd be shocked, but
the truth is I think bugs are basically for stomping.*

*Anyway, in two days we are supposed to be in Obala and then
it is just another day's trek—isn't that a wonderful word!—to the
wasp colony. Wish me luck. Your intrepid explorer,*
Eve.

The town of Obala was, as Dr. Harper had expected, less
hospitable than the jungle. Stray, hunger-maddened dogs
roamed the dirt streets and ragged loungers passed the time
by pitching rocks at the mongrels. A barracks, created during an enterprising dictator's regime, had been roughly con-
verted into a hotel. The room Dr. Harper rented was the
most minimal of sleeping compartments, with two cots, a
broken window that had been repaired with cardboard and

tape, a dresser missing one drawer, and a frail, lopsided wooden chair that no prudent person would ever sit on. The last tenant had left an empty vodka bottle on the floor in the middle of the room.

"Not four stars," Dr. Harper said.

"I think it's quaint," his daughter said, patting his shoulder.

"Yes, and Charles Manson is cute," her father said. "Well, let's get our stuff in here, and then I'll set about devising a real lock for this door. This looks like the perfect place for having one's throat cut."

Dr. Harper did not have a high opinion of his fellow man. The worst part of these expeditions, which had comprised the better part of his summers for the last twelve years, consisted of his interaction with the humanity that inhabited these regions. There was a law of nature at work here. Wherever a delightful and exotic insect dwelt, there also dwelt—often in military garb—vile, untrustworthy men.

For this reason—among many other excellent reasons—he had been reluctant to bring Eve. The plan had been to show her some of the cities on the coast and then send her back to Boston. His daughter had known, however, that he was defenseless when it came to her whims, and she had decided to stay. She always won in these battles of will.

At least this was not to be an arduous expedition. The country was in a period of relative tranquility and prosperity.

That night Dr. Harper and his daughter ate at a restaurant that was surprisingly clean and well-regulated. The food was excellent, and the proprietress, a large woman in a black dress, saw to it that their wine glasses remained filled and that they were served in a timely, elegant fashion.

The only disruptive element was the appearance, midway through the meal, of a fat man wearing a blue polo shirt and khaki slacks. This man, middle-aged and balding, was accompanied by a short, unhappy woman and a young man, equally gloomy, whose disgusted and bored expression declared that he was in the company of his parents.

The fat man was one of those individuals who seem to revel in abrasiveness. He complained loudly, urging his fellow diners to observe how ill-used he was. "What sort of a wine is this?" he bellowed. "What sort of a fool do they think I am? Do they think I'd actually drink this?"

Ordinarily, this sort of behavior would have been easily ignored by Dr. Harper, who didn't expect much of his fellows. But it was not lost on Dr. Harper that the native customers were all observing this man with polite distaste. It also occurred to Dr. Harper that this man, so obviously American, was a fellow countryman and might, therefore, seem representative. That Dr. Harper might find himself grouped, in the local mind, with this offensive bumpkin irritated the professor and kept him from the full enjoyment of his meal.

On leaving, Dr. Harper was complimenting his hostess at length—and she was beaming mightily—when a meaty hand was clasped on his shoulder.

"My God, an American! It's good to see a white face."

Dr. Harper turned.

"Bob Gentry," the man said, and waving a hand, he introduced his wife and son, who were tucked behind him like rueful mendicants in the shadow of their lord. "Harriet and Kurt."

Reluctantly, Dr. Harper introduced himself and his daughter.

Gentry leaned forward and narrowed his eyes. "You are not Dr. Philip 'Hymenoptera' Harper, are you? You are not the man who wrote 'Sexual Specific Mound Building in Select *Formicinae*'?"

Dr. Harper admitted that he was.

Gentry slapped him on the back. "Damned small planet, Harper. I'm Dr. Robert Gentry. Spiders. You may have seen my article on adaptive coloration and mating behavior in *Migidae* in *Modern Arachnid* last month."

"I don't have much time to read outside my field," Dr. Harper said. No sense in encouraging the man.

"Of course, of course," Gentry said, continuing to thump Harper on the back. "The social insects are the stars of entomology. The rest of us are in their shadow."

Dr. Harper found himself at a table drinking a glass of wine while Gentry talked. The man was an incredible braggart, and seemed to have published a number of articles in popular, even sensational, journals—if, in fact, he were to be believed.

Mrs. Gentry seemed bored, perhaps drunk, and Dr. Harper was surprised to discover that she was attending to what her husband said. "That was in Yablis," she would suddenly say. "The flies were awful, awful." Then grim silence would overtake her again.

Out of the corner of his eye, Dr. Harper noticed that his daughter and the pale young man who was Gentry's son were chatting easily, leaning toward each other across the table. Occasionally his daughter would laugh, with her sharp, over-loud bark that had jumped a generation from his own father. *At least*, Harper thought, *she is enjoying herself.*

This Gentry fellow was proving to be an opinionated, condescending bore who seemed to possess some personal antipathy toward wasps and bees and ants—those creatures that Dr. Harper had devoted his life to.

"This hive stuff bores me sick," Gentry said. "A lot of bullshit." The man leaned forward and clutched Dr. Harper's shoulder. "Wolf spiders are the magnificent lords of the grass," Gentry said. "Solitary, ruthless predators."

Dr. Harper rose, disengaging himself from the man's grip, and protested that he had an early rising ahead of him and needed his sleep.

"As do I," Dr. Gentry laughed. "Perhaps we'll see each other in the fields."

"Perhaps," Dr. Harper said, confident that the jungles around Obala were sufficiently vast to prevent it.

In the morning, Dr. Harper woke feeling ill, head pounding, mouth parched. Only the thought of escaping Obala and the self-satisfied Gentry could compel him to rise. But once up and moving, he began to feel better.

In the bathroom down the hall, a large and hirsute spider crouched in the shower stall. Dr. Harper removed a sandal and whacked the spider with it. The spider made a satisfying sound, like spit on a hot griddle, and Harper scraped it down the drain. He felt oddly triumphant.

Dear Janey—

Just a quick note. The porters are on their way back to Obala within the hour, and I want this letter to go with them. It is always iffy whether these letters will make it or not. The postage stamp is not powerful magic in these parts.

We have arrived at our destination (I love that sentence, and I think, really, it is why I wanted to come all the way with Father). Father now spends the better part of every day sitting out in this field with his camera and a whole necklace of lenses. The field is pocked with sandy mounds and all these things that, at first, you might think were big dragonflies. They are wasps, yellow spotted, low-flying, spider-stinging wasps. Dozens of them dart over the tall grass.

This is your natural history lesson for the day, so don't doze off or stick your tongue in Tommy's ear when you are supposed to be reading MY LETTER. Okay. These big wasps—the females— spend all their time looking for spiders, and when they see a spider they swoop down on it and sting it and then lay their eggs on it and take it back to the burrow.

Here's the yucky part—yeah, I know, it is all sort of semi-yucky: the spider isn't dead. The spider is just paralyzed, so that when the wasp larva hatches it has fresh food. Gross, right?

That's the end of that natural history lesson, and I will now proceed to my own natural history—which is far more interesting.

I have met this terrific guy, Kurt, who is down here with his parents. His father is also an entomologist. We only met briefly, but I was smitten. I think love is a sort of karmic thing, and not a function of time anyway. Like you might love someone because you knew him in a previous reincarnation. Anyway, he has got these great black eyelashes and this sweet smile and he is very funny and charming and about four million times more sensitive than Mr. Mark "Football & Beer" Buckley.

I could tell he liked me too, despite the fact that I look like a mosquito's idea of a pizza these days. We are going to try to see each other again. I told him what I knew, which was that Father was going off to study a famous—well, among entomologists—wasp colony, and Kurt said his father would know where that was. So Kurt is going to try to steer his parents in our direction so he can see me.

I hope he can do it. There isn't a whole hell of a lot else going on. I'm not about to complain, because Father will just say I didn't have to come and that, in fact, I insisted on coming. Father is your basic I-told-you-so personality, so much so that it is a sickness with him, and I'm not going to give him that satisfaction.

This place has it moments anyway. Yesterday it rained like crazy in the morning and then, when it stopped, these huge mists rolled in, like something in a dream, and the trees seemed to stretch all the way to the sky and I probably could have climbed right up to the giant's castle and stolen the golden goose except I'm scared of heights. Anyway, it was heavy-duty beautiful.

Your jungle correspondent—Eve.

Kurt Gentry had never written a poem before, and it wasn't coming along too great. "Your eyes are like slices of heaven," he wrote. Kurt stopped writing and flopped on his back.

His circle of vision consisted of blue sky invaded by gnarled tree limbs with bulbous, waxy leaves. He sat up again and regarded his father, who was fifty or sixty feet away in tall, yellow grass. The old man hunched over a tripod-mounted camera like a paunchy, inept assassin waiting for a minor dignitary. He was, Kurt knew, actually waiting for a spider to pop out of a little silver-dollar-sized trap door made of sod and devour some unwary beetle. It was an odd thing for a grown man to wait on. This sort of parental activity had convinced Kurt, long ago, to pursue a career in business administration and one day get a job in an air-conditioned office where the only bugs were in your computer program. Kurt was accompanying his parents this year because—dismally—the alternative had been summer school and a job at the Qwik Mart.

He stopped watching his father—a dull pastime if ever there were one—and turned to watch his mother who had just come out of the tent and was fixing dinner. She was wearing a large, yellow sunhat and a blue dress that contained enough material for two dresses and touched the tops of her worn boots.

As usual, his mother's industry and domesticity irritated Kurt, drove him wild in fact. He envisioned soaking her in the lighter fluid that she was presently sprinkling over charcoal and setting her on fire. This is not to say that he did not love her; he did. But there was something about her that sucked the excitement from all things surrounding her. Like anti-gravity, except this was anti-adventure. Like a human black hole that gathered all the light rays of possibility and bent them into one narrow path.

If Indiana Jones had traveled with my mother, Kurt thought, *nothing would ever have happened.*

This thought presented itself with such bleak conviction that Kurt flinched away from it and returned to the poem he was writing.

"Your eyes are like slices of heaven, your lips glisten as though you have just eaten a cherry popsicle."

Kurt's friend Mort "Waxy" Baker had said that poetry was the best way to get chicks. "Poetry excites their erotic centers," Waxy had said.

Kurt was quickly coming to the conclusion that poetry was beyond him. He would have to rely on alcohol. He would steal some of his father's bourbon and get her drunk on Cokes and bourbon.

That is, of course, if he ever saw her again. *My god, she might be lost to me forever.* This thought made him sick. "Eve," he groaned, and he stretched his hands to the sky.

Lying on his back under the shade of the tree, he grew drowsy and may actually have been sleeping when his father leaned over him and said, "If I was a vulture, I would have snapped your eyes out."

It was Kurt's opinion that his father's laughter, more of a bellow really, should have been subject to stiff fines if not actual physical punishment—whipping perhaps.

At dinner Kurt asked, as casually as possible, if his father was aware of the wasp colony that was the subject of Dr. Harper's interest.

"As a matter of fact," his father said, "we are going there tomorrow. I have a hunch that the greatest concentration of *Cyclosomia tantalus* will be found in that same area."

So delighted was Kurt by these words, that he felt expansive, oddly benevolent, and so—in an unprecedented display of interest—asked his father what a *Cyclosomia tantalus* was.

"A damned beautiful trap-door spider. Big fellows. Very striking patterns. Endangered species. I'd love to get them on video. Jesus, wouldn't Wilson turn green with envy! I guess that would kick his *Loxoceles* out of the limelight for awhile."

Kurt nodded his head as his father extolled the virtues of *C. tantalus*. "Eve," Kurt thought (for poetry is addictive), "your eyes are like high-priced blue jewels."

Dr. Harper was content to sit in the folding chair and let the wasps dart by at the level of his knees. They were such lordly creatures. They moved through the air like fighter jets, and when they alighted in the sand, their wings ticked with clockwork precision as though an elegant arrangement of tiny gears locked limb and thorax and wing into one smooth-functioning unit.

Competition in the insect world made the battle for survival amid higher animals look positively cozy by comparison. These large female wasps killed spiders to feed to their young. Think of it: predator against predator, like lions feeding on wolves. And the wasps had their own enemies: Small clouds of satellite flies would hover over a wasp returning to its burrow, hoping to deposit their young on the spider carcass. The larval satellite fly would then devour both spider and wasp eggs.

The battles that raged in this sandy quarter-mile of grassland affected Dr. Harper's mood and made him feel a certain ruthlessness and satisfaction in his own accomplishments. He had done well and if, occasionally, it had been at the expense of his colleagues, then he was not about to apologize for obeying what was a first principle of existence. And if his fellow entomologists didn't understand such things, then they had failed to learn the lessons of their profession.

"Hallooo!" a voice shouted, and Dr. Harper turned and squinted into the trees. A man in a pith helmet was standing at the edge of the trees and waving. Behind him two other figures stood.

"Good God," Dr. Harper muttered. "It's Gentry."

Dear Janey—

Kurt and I have been reunited! Yes. And that karma thing I told you about is true. How else would fate have conspired—another great word, huh?—to bring us back together? You see, Kurt's dad is studying a particular kind of trap-door spider that likes the same sort of sandy, open ground that Father's wasps like. So Kurt's dad just naturally had to come here. You can say that is just coincidence if you want to, but I know better.

Kurt is a dear. He wrote me a poem that is sooooo romantic. There is a river not far from here, and we go there for picnics and stuff. Last time we were there, these neon-green birds came and sat in the tree branches. It was awesome.

We are getting to know each other pretty well—wink, wink— but I haven't sorted out all my feelings yet—like what about Mr. Mark "No Foreplay" Buckley back home? I will keep you posted. So far I have retained my virtue, but I'm pretty sure I am in love with Kurt.

This letter isn't going anywhere. There aren't any mailmen in these parts. So I will just add to it and send it when I can. Later.

Bob Gentry tossed off his drink, wiped the sweat from his forehead and said to his wife: "If that inbred New England bastard talks down his nose to me one more time, I'm gonna stick his head up his ass."

"Dear," Mrs. Gentry said, "I don't know why you dislike

Dr. Harper so much. Why, you two are colleagues. I would think that you would enjoy each other's company."

"Hah," Gentry said, pouring himself another drink. "Did you see how he acted when we arrived? He acted like this was his goddam exclusive country club and who the fuck were we? I tell you, Harriet, the social insect crowd with their grants and their goddam theories and their goddam bee dances and petty head counts . . . there is something missing in those people and that's what attracts them to fucking ants and bees. It's a drone mentality."

Mrs. Gentry, who had heard it all before, sighed. "Yes dear, I'm sure you're right."

"Where's Kurt?" Gentry asked.

"I have no idea," his wife said.

Gentry frowned. "Trying to get into that girl's pants, if I know our Kurt," Gentry muttered.

Mrs. Gentry said, "I'm sure you're right, dear."

The next morning, Gentry almost broke his neck tripping over the rope.

"What the fuck?" he roared. He stood up, brushed the yellow dust from his trousers, and looked around. "Harper," he said. "Goddam Harper."

He was right, of course.

"Yes," Dr. Harper said when a red-faced Gentry tracked him down. "I've taken the liberty of roping off a section. I need to make a study of the wasp population, and I need to establish boundaries."

"Your fucking 'boundaries' almost killed me. Didn't it occur to you to warn people?" Gentry paused. "You know, you are kind of an asshole, Harper."

Dr. Harper stiffened. He was tall—with a good six inches on Gentry—and now he looked down at the shorter man with an expression of cool disdain. "There was no one to warn when I arrived here," Harper said. "I frankly did not expect a lot of tourists to arrive and despoil this site."

"Tourists?"

"Perhaps you prefer 'travel writer' or 'nature enthusiast.' In any event, your arrival was not anticipated."

"Maybe you haven't anticipated eating that dustball under your nose."

Gentry swung at Harper, who stepped back. Gentry missed and stumbled forward. Harper planted the palms of his hands on Gentry's chest and shoved Gentry, who sat down heavily in the dust.

"Father!" Eve screamed, running across the field. "What's going on?" As her father turned to address her, Gentry gathered himself into a crouch and rushed forward, catching the taller man below the knees and tackling him.

"Son-of-a-bitch!" Dr. Harper screamed.

As they rolled in the dirt, Eve screamed again. An unusual number of wasps seemed to buzz about, as though attracted to the brawling pair.

I think, Eve continued in her letter to her friend Janey, *the wasps may have been interested in the outcome. After all, even one professor would feed a hell of a lot of baby wasps.*

Anyway, Kurt and Mrs. Gentry heard the commotion, and together we separated them. But gosh, Janey, it's all rotten luck. I wish they'd stop this feud. Things were going great with Kurt and me and now our parents say we aren't to go near each other.

It's not my fault they can't get along. I'm not responsible for that. And neither is Kurt. Fortunately, Father is a heavy sleeper and Kurt says his dad gets loaded every night and would sleep through a firefight. So there's hope.

It was actually pretty exciting creeping through the dark, hoping she wouldn't step on a branch and wake her father.

And it was dangerous too. Everyone knew that the worst sort of animals prowled at night. Some ravenous jungle carnivore might get her. She might step on a snake. This jungle had snakes so poisonous that they made an encounter with a cobra seem no worse than a bad sunburn—by comparison.

Eve's heart beat loudly. Far off, a pack of dogs barked—only they weren't dogs. Her father said they were monkeys. Nearer to hand, a weird bird—or maybe a frog—uttered a wheezy *what-the-hell, what-the-hell.*

And now she could hear the sound of the river.

"Kurt," she whispered. "Kurt, where are you?"

"Eve," Kurt whispered.

"Eek!" Eve said, jumping. He could have reached out and touched her. He was that close.

He took her in his arms and kissed her. She kissed him back.

"Isn't it awful," Eve said, feeling dizzy with tragedy.

"It's rotten," Kurt said, sticking his tongue in her mouth.

"I love you," Eve said.

"I also love you," Kurt said. "I brought the blanket," he added.

In the days that followed, Gentry found it wasn't that difficult to avoid Harper. Indeed, if Gentry were careful, he could go a whole day without glimpsing that man's gaunt, unpleasant form. The trick was not to look in the direction of the roped-off area.

I refuse to give him another thought, Gentry thought, and while that was the ideal rather than the actuality, Gentry did manage to get on with his work, that of observing the extraordinary *Cyclosomia tantalus.* And these large spiders were so enchanting, such fascinating companions, that they often made Gentry forget that anything else existed.

A particularly large spider, grey with blue markings, had

come to hold a special place in his heart. He called this spider Alexander and spent many hours studying him.

Alexander was an older spider, and cautious. He would spend hours beneath his trap door, the lid just barely raised, and anything out of the ordinary would cause the door to slam shut and remain so for many hours—an entire day on two occasions.

Gentry longed for a better look at this specimen, and so set about providing a variety of insects for Alexander. It was no small task winning the spider's confidence, but Gentry—like all entomologists—was a patient man.

In time, Alexander would emerge halfway from his burrow at Gentry's approach. No doubt the spider could recognize his provider's footfalls.

Gentry had only to drop a beetle on the ground, and Alexander was out of his burrow, upon the arthropod, and gone again in the blink of an eye.

This was still unsatisfactory, and Gentry devised a plan for keeping Alexander in the open. Later the professor was to savagely reproach himself for not heeding an internal voice that, even then, suggested that there was something ignoble in abusing the spider's trust.

But science is a cruel master, and Gentry had to obey. Taking a piece of thread, he tied one of the beetle's legs to a large nail.

"Hello, Alexander," he said, approaching the spider who, as usual, offered a view of spined mandibles and forelegs from under his plug of sod. Gentry leaned down and thrust the nail into the ground, then sat back. Alexander launched himself from beneath his trap door, grabbed the beetle, and was stopped dead in his race back to his burrow by the thread attached to nail and beetle.

What a magnificent specimen, Gentry thought.

And then, almost casually, tragedy struck. A giant, yellow wasp, one of the many that had become such a part of the scenery that Gentry had easily forgotten them, landed on Alexander and stung him.

"God," Gentry screamed, and he reached forward and whacked the insect off Alexander's back. The wasp struggled to regain its balance, and Gentry crushed it under a boot. "Aaaaaah," he said.

"Alexander . . ." he said, turning back to the spider.

But it was too late. The wasp's powerful toxin had already done its work, and Alexander was on his back, his legs drawn up in a final convulsion—for all the world like a severed fist.

"Are you all right, dear?" his wife asked him that night. He could not answer and instead drank more heavily than usual.

"Murderer," he thought, reproaching himself. Alexander had had a reason for his haste. The poor fellow had been surrounded by assassins.

Gentry cursed himself for being so blind. He had known that Dr. Harper's damnable wasps preyed on spiders.

Later that night, Mrs. Gentry, noting her husband's black mood and frenzied drinking, repeated the question: "Are you all right, dear?"

Gentry replied. "He thinks he can just run roughshod over us. Well, he can't."

It was damned perplexing. Dr. Harper didn't know what to make of it. He dissected another of the dead wasps. This one had been missing a part of its head. There were predators that preyed on these wasps—robber flies among them—but he hadn't observed any in the area.

Two days before he had begun finding the bodies. Often they were in the process of being dismembered by ants, so it was difficult to establish what sort of injury had initially killed them. Maybe it was some sort of internal parasite. If so, Dr. Harper had found no trace of it, no clue.

That very evening, he discovered the cause. Feeling disheartened, he had left the field in the afternoon, around three perhaps, and retired to his tent to sleep. But he could not sleep in the heat of the day, and the mystery of the dying wasps troubled him. He rose and returned to the field and there, as bold as any Times Square hooker on a slow night, stood the despicable Gentry, air rifle in hand, blithely firing away at the wasps. Even as Harper watched, a wasp that had just landed on a sandy mound was neatly decapitated to the accompaniment of the gun's softly innocent *phutt!*

"What do you think you are doing!" Harper shouted.

Gentry jumped, turned and regarded Harper. The merest ghost of guilt departed from the fat man's features, and he smiled evilly. "Popping the little bastards," he said. "Sending them to hell."

Dr. Harper roared and launched himself at the fat man.

By the time you get this it will be nothing but a catalog of horrors. We may all be dead in which case I guess you will never get this letter.

Oh Janey, it's awful. We are at war. Father caught Dr. Gentry shooting the wasps! Yes. With an air rifle! Can you imagine! Anyway, Father got the gun away from Dr. Gentry and hit him with it. Gave him a good crack on the side of the head, and Dr. Gentry did not come around immediately.

Things are getting worse. Father feared that Dr. Gentry's mental condition might lead to some sort of life-threatening reprisal, so Father acted while Dr. Gentry was still out.

Father has taken a number of spiders hostage. Yes. Father has this collecting vacuum gun. It looks a little like a dust buster, you

*know, one of those hand-held vacuum cleaners. It sucks bugs up and
deposits them in a canister.*

*Father went all over the field finding the trap-door burrows and
sucking up their contents. He presently has about ten spiders in jars.*

*Mrs. Gentry acts as the go-between in all this, carrying messages
between Father and Dr. Gentry.*

*Father thinks I should search her before she enters our tent. "She
isn't exactly a neutral party," he says, but I have refused to do any
searches.*

*This is crazy, isn't it, Janey? Kurt says that we should not let
it affect our relationship, but I don't know how it can fail to. I
mean, I feel a little like a traitor when I slip off to see Kurt. But
I do it.*

What next?

It was quite possible, Gentry thought, that he was dying.
The blow that Dr. Harper had dealt him had left Gentry
altered. Perhaps, at this very moment, some slow drifting
clot of blood was floating into the backwaters of his brain
where it would detonate and scatter the thoughts and dreams
and identity of Bob Gentry.

In any event, he felt weak, and was forced to retreat to his
sleeping bag. This was an ignoble state of affairs, but he
reminded himself that all great men had endured hardships.

"What?" he asked his wife, sitting up quickly and immediately regretting the impulse as a wave of nausea and vertigo
engulfed him. "He has what?"

"Hostages," his wife said. "I believe if you could just reas-
sure him that you will not retaliate. He does say that it was
an accident. He says he was trying to take the rifle away from
you, that's all."

Gentry lay back. With some dignity, he said, "The blow
was deliberate. There was malice aforethought, Harriet, and

52

plenty. But forget that. My mind is still clouded. Are you telling me that that cretinous bastard is holding specimens of *Cyclosomia* hostage? What kind of madman are we dealing with? *Cyclosomia tantalus* is an endangered species!"

"Yes, dear," Mrs. Gentry said. "Although I don't think he would actually kill them. I mean, I believe he is frightened for his own personal safety."

"He's right to be," Gentry grumbled. "I'm going to kill him."

"I do wish you wouldn't talk like that," Mrs. Gentry said.

That night, Kurt and Eve commiserated in each other's arms. "Our lives have been ruined by the stupidity of our elders," Eve said.

"I love you," Kurt said. He slid a hand down her back and under the elastic waistband of her jeans.

"I love you too," Eve said. "But what are we going to do?"

The river gurgled and the monkeys barked, all unaware of human strife.

"There's nothing we can do," Kurt said. His hand was feeling sort of numb, as though it had fallen asleep. "And your dad and my dad aren't the kind of people who budge. They are both as stubborn as mud turtles."

"Then it's up to us," Eve said, breaking away. "Come on. And don't make a sound."

Her father had shown her where the trip wires were, the flashbulb triggers and trashcan deadfalls. "Step over this wire," she told Kurt. *Was this betrayal?* she wondered.

The thought kept coming into her mind, and each time she methodically shooed it away. Someone had to act. Someone had to demonstrate some good faith.

Still, she felt terrible when she gazed at her father's sleeping form before reaching past him and lifting the first of the jars from behind his head. She was, after all, his daughter, and there was no doubt that he would see this as the vilest treachery.

Moving with dreadful slowness, she passed the jars back to Kurt, who wrapped each one in a towel or t-shirt before easing it into the sack.

Once her father coughed in his sleep and muttered something. Eve's heart stopped. She almost dropped the jar she was holding. But somehow she endured, and the last jar disappeared into the sack.

"I'll come with you," she whispered, when they were back in the night and well away from her father's tent.

"No, better not," Kurt said. "I'll talk to him; I'll tell Dad we want peace, and then come back and tell you how it went. Okay?"

"Okay," Eve said. She hugged him again. "I love you."

"Me too," he said and was gone.

And he did love her. Oh she was beautiful, more beautiful than the stars or the crappy poetry he had written her. She was beautiful right to her soul, and brave and noble.

As Kurt hoisted the bag of spiders over his shoulder, he realized he did not deserve her. He knew he couldn't have done what she had just done.

Well, he would do his part. He hurried on, keeping the flashlight's beam low to the ground, following its pale grey circle of illuminated grass.

"Dad," he whispered, leaning down and peering in the tent. He could make out his mother's frazzled hair above the rumpled sheet, but his father's sleeping bag was empty.

Maybe he's taking a leak, Kurt thought, and he lay the sack down and went in search of his errant sire.

But his father was not in the immediate vicinity, and with a sense of growing dread, Kurt walked out into the fields.

He saw him then—or what had to be him, a stooped figure in the roped-off area. Kurt shouted, but clapped his mouth shut on the shout, realizing that the last thing he wanted was to wake Dr. Harper.

The truncated shout was enough to send the man in the fields running, and Kurt ran after him. But Kurt forgot the staked rope, and it sent him sailing, effortlessly. He executed a belly flop in the sand and the flashlight rolled across the ground.

Crawling on his knees, he patted the ground. There! But no, it wasn't the flashlight, merely an empty can. Discarding it, he continued to blindly feel for the flashlight. Ah! He clutched it, flicked the switch. It still worked. He played the beam over the ground. A white, powdery dust covered the sand. *What's this?*, he wondered. The beam fell on the cylindrical can that, for a moment, had fooled him into thinking it was a flashlight. He lifted it up and read the label. The skull and crossbones said it all, and before he had identified the poison and its use, he understood.

"Great Dad, just great. *Shit.*"

Kurt stood up. Tears puffed into his eyes. Eve had tried so damned hard, so goddam hard and brave and all for goddam nothing. I mean, this was fucking unforgivable.

Wait, Kurt thought, *maybe it isn't too late. Maybe I can scoff this poison back up before it kills the wasps.*

Kurt got down on his knees and began using his hands to scrape the powder back into the empty can. *Why not? Why not?*

The first wasp stung Kurt on the cheek, and then, as though they had agreed upon some silent signal, a dozen wasps stung him on the neck and face and on his hands.

"Aaaaaah," Kurt said, standing up. He felt dizzy, suddenly

chilled. He took a step forward and fell to his knees. *Just great*, he thought.

Oh Janey. I am leaving this letter where father can find it. I have no reason to go on living. My Kurt is dead. I went looking for him and I found him. I have returned to my tent just long enough to record these last words and then I will slip into Father's room for the last time in my life. I will steal a bottle of wine he keeps in his trunk, and I will steal the pills that are always within his reach in case he cannot sleep.

I don't know what happened. I think the wasps killed Kurt somehow. I guess it's that damned karma I always talk about. We tried to set things right. I gave the hostage spiders back. But it was too late. It was always too late. We were doomed.

I want you to have all my tapes and CDs. You have been a good friend. Love always, Eve.

Dr. Harper, awakening early and discovering the theft of the spiders, bolted from his tent. In his haste, he set off one of the trip wires and was rewarded with a crackle of flashbulbs.

"Jesus," Harper growled.

He pushed off across the field, his one thought to have Gentry's throat between his hands. And then he saw them.

The boy lay sprawled on his back, and Eve lay with her head on his chest. Dr. Harper's first thought was that he had surprised the teenagers in a sexual liaison, but he was immediately disabused of this notion by the dread stillness of the couple and the abstract and impersonal angle of Kurt Gentry's head.

"Oh my God!" Harper screamed.

Dear Janey—
I am not dead after all. Neither is Kurt. Wasp stings depress

breathing, and Father had some adrenalin along for just such an emergency. We both looked pretty dead, I guess. It unsettled Father. He still looks sort of astonished.

I'm not dead, so the deal is off about the tapes and the CDs. Sorry.

I drank a whole bottle of wine and swallowed a bottle of vitamin C.

Hey, the light was lousy in my father's tent. But my heart was in the right place.

I am glad anyway that tragedy was avoided. Kurt is doing fine, although he moves sort of slowly and occasionally forgets his name. The doctors say this will pass. Dr. Gentry and Father have not, however, reconciled. Lawsuits are on the horizon if the Entomologists' Arbitration League fails in its efforts to reconcile our parents— and I believe it will fail.

I'm looking forward to the new semester, how about you? Tell Mark that if he wants to meet my train it will be arriving on September second at two in the afternoon. Don't say I told you. Just say it would be a nice surprise. Love,

Eve.

The Return of Count Electric

1

Two weeks after my mother died, I received a letter from Harriet Goddard, my mother's best friend. The letter was a brief note of commiseration. She apologized for failing to attend the funeral. She had been prevented by extreme ill-health and had had to exert all her efforts toward postponing her own funeral through the use of folk remedies and bed rest. Weakened but recovering, Mrs. Goddard was now taking the opportunity to write. She included a sealed letter my mother had entrusted to her nine years ago.

"Frankly," Mrs. Goddard wrote, "I had forgotten the existence of this letter, only coming upon it two days ago in a book of photos which I had Will bring down from the attic."

I ceased reading Harriet's letter to heft my mother's sealed envelope in my hand. "Mark Pearson!" she had written. The exclamation point after my name was characteristic of my mother. She had been a shrill, exclamatory woman. The envelope was yellow—not the result of age but rather my mother's delight in brightly colored stationery—and bulky. It filled me with misgivings. I do not like surprises. I yearn for order and cleanliness. Even as a child I hated Christmas, all those damnable gifts, those gaudy secrets. I like a thing to be forthright about what it is, not hidden in wrapping paper covered with elves. No telling what is inside. All that prettiness could hide something really horrible: a knot of snakes, perhaps.

So I looked at this sealed envelope and considered throwing it away unopened. Mrs. Goddard seemed to advise doing just that. "No doubt," she had written, "your mother forgot—just as I did—the existence of this letter. Had she remembered, she might have asked me to destroy it long ago. She gave it to me when she was living briefly with us, having just separated from your father. You were living in Los Angeles or San Francisco—someplace in California—and I know your mother felt quite alone in the world. It is not easy to leave a man you have lived with for forty years, and she was deeply depressed. I suspect that the letter was written in despair and may even—poor Lila!—be a sort of suicide note.

"I hope it will not cause you any pain—I am still not certain I am doing the right thing in sending it along—and I urge you to consider that it was written nine years ago during difficult times."

Damning curiosity, I ripped the letter open. No snakes. I discovered a two-page letter and a dozen or so newspaper clippings. I blinked at the newsprint. The dry phrases of objective journalism rose up like steam. . . . *had been missing for three days. Police refused to comment . . . abrasions and puncture wounds. Death however appears to be the result of electrical shock . . . very high voltage . . . electrocuted. Similarities in all four deaths suggest a single killer. Dorothy Simpson, who police and newspapers are now describing as Count Electric's seventh victim, was last seen . . .*

I turned to my mother's note. "Mark," it began, like a shout from the back door. "Dear God, help me, I think your father is Count Electric!"

I laughed out loud, got up and went to the window. My apartment overlooked the beltway, and the last of the rush hour traffic grimly poured out of Washington, headlights anticipating the dark. It was seven in the evening and I had spent the day writing a proposal for a government contract. I had, in other words, spent the day lying, inflating the credentials of people who probably wouldn't even be available for the project and "implementing" this and "facilitating" that and generally trying to give the impression that we were the sort of pretentious, bureaucratic sycophants that the Defense department would enjoy doing business with. It was exhausting work and had put me in a black mood. My mother's opening sentence, so like my mother in its sense of breathless revelation, instantly cheered me.

I thought about my father. The funeral was the first time I had seen him in over a year. He looked somehow fraudulent in a suit, for in my mind he is always wearing green slacks and a tan shirt with the logo of the air conditioning and heating company he worked for. I went over and spoke to him. There were tears in his eyes, and he looked much older than when I had last seen him. He wore a scarf too, which seemed unwarranted. It was a balmy April afternoon. We had talked about the loveliness of the flowers, the blessing of a quick, as opposed to lingering, death, etc.

Now I tried to imagine my father as Count Electric, Fairfax's most diabolical serial killer, a madman who killed at least eight women in the course of two years. I couldn't do it.

I had not visited my father since his retirement to Waterford, a small Northern Virginia town perhaps fifty miles outside of Washington, D.C. and of some vague historical significance.

I returned to the sofa and picked up my mother's nine-year old revelation and read on. To her credit, she too had some difficulty with the concept of old Harry Pearson as serial murderer and pervert. I say pervert because the newspaper accounts, although vague, suggested that the murderer was driven by warped and hideously inverted sexual impulses. The women who fell afoul of Count Electric were discovered bound and naked. They had been electrocuted. They had also been the victims of some sexual outrage that had inspired one homicide investigator to say, "We are dealing with a very deviant personality. A very sick character." When asked to comment further, the man had merely shaken his head.

My father was not inclined to show his true feelings. He was frugal with his inner self. Aside from announcing every evening that he was "beat," "whupped" or "goddam exhausted," he didn't keep us posted on his spiritual and emotional life. We were largely in the dark with my father—but it didn't seem such an impenetrable darkness that a Count Electric could have crouched in it without our noticing. My father simply wasn't enough of an actor to hide such a personality. Then too, the notes that Count Electric began leaving at the scenes of his crimes seemed utterly foreign to my father's nature. Those notes that the press had chosen to reveal were always signed Count Electric and were in quotes, like blurbs from movie reviews. "Stimulating!" a note might read. Or: "A powerful experience. Electrifying!" Or, my favorite: "A shocking, Post-Modern expression of technological alienation." These notes were typed on three-by-five index cards and left on the victims' bare stomachs. It was easier imagining my father as a murderer than as the writer of such notes, and my mother seemed to share that view.

My mother had discovered the newspaper clippings in a dusty suitcase in the toolshed. She rarely visited that spider-haunted refuge for rusting lawnmowers, broken-toothed saws, air conditioning parts and lumber, but, in a frenzied search for gardening gloves, she had left no stone unturned, no suitcase unopened, and so she had come upon the clippings.

Her discovery occurred in 1983. The murders themselves, never solved, occurred in 1976 and '77. Apparently the clippings had lain in hiding for six years.

Well, it seemed to me that my mother was taking a rather large leap here, from her husband's possessing gruesome newspaper clippings to her husband's being the subject of those clippings. A fascination with serial killers is not unusual—books on the subject do a brisk business—and I assumed my father was simply indulging a furtive hobby.

I should have given my mother more credit. I read on. "I know what you are thinking," her note said. "You are thinking your mother is overreacting. You may even be shaking your head in that superior way that makes you appear retarded." No, it was the machine that filled her with dread. She was unable to describe it precisely. It was "evil, spiderlike"; the electric cord coming out of it was "like a devil's tail." She thought there might be blood on some of the needles although of course it could have been rust. The machine bristled with needles. It was obscene, pornographic. She didn't like thinking about it.

The suitcase that held the clippings also contained this infernal machine, this *proof* of my father's guilt. I was less convinced, knowing my mother for a woman who saw all machines as menacing and alien.

The rest of my mother's letter consisted of some fancy wrestling with her conscience. Should she call the police? Should she keep silent? On reflection, she conceded that my father might not be Count Electric. The machine might not be a killing machine. It could all prove embarrassing. And no killings had occurred in six years . . . Eventually a dread of public humiliation and scandal conquered her moral ambivalence, and she wrote this letter rather than go to the police. The letter ended dramatically: "Pray your father is an innocent man! I would rather be a foolish, paranoid old woman than the wife of a murderer!" Obviously, she never did contact the police, but her doubts were sufficient to make her leave the old man.

I put the letter and newspaper clippings in a desk drawer and went into the kitchen to fix myself dinner. Later that night I called my father. I think he was surprised to hear from me. His voice had the wary tone of a man expecting to be asked for money. We managed to talk for about fifteen awkward minutes, and by the end of the conversation I had a half-hearted invitation to drop by.

After the telephone conversation, I went into the living room and listened to Beethoven. I drank some wine and thought how nice it would be if my father were, in fact, Count Electric. I could see my secretary looking at me differently when I replied, "Yes, it's true. My father is Count Electric." How exactly would I say it? I think I would sigh, look vaguely disgusted, produce a rueful smile as if to say, "One's stuck with one's family, isn't one?"

At around ten that evening the phone rang. It was Elizabeth reminding me that we were having dinner with John and Elaine on Saturday.

"I don't know," I said.

"Mark, what do you mean you don't know?"

"I told my father I'd come out on Saturday."

"Mark. Really, you can be so thoughtless."

"I'm not thoughtless," I said. "My mother just died. Wanting to see my father in the wake of such an event can hardly be called thoughtless."

That silenced her. We talked for awhile about the office, and then I told her I would see her on Monday and hung up. Elizabeth is all right, but unless I am very much mistaken, she wants to have sex with me and that isn't going to happen.

I woke that Saturday with the old numbness gripping my left side. I couldn't feel my foot when it touched the floor. But moving around, shaving, making coffee, I began to feel better. The migraine failed to materialize and by the time I was on the road I was feeling fine.

2

My father was, of course, surprised to see me on his doorstep, but he accepted my arrival with good grace, even managed a smile although I caught an expression closer to dismay when I glanced in the hall mirror.

It was a tidy little house, brick, pretty much what I would have expected. My father had developed an enthusiasm for gardening that surprised me, and as punishment for popping in on him, he took me out in the garden and talked about plants and fertilizers and the weather. All the while the sun hissed overhead like a frying egg, and a yellow jacket buzzed around my mouth seeking entrance, as though I were a magic grotto full of honey. It was unpleasant, and when we got back inside I found the cool shade of the sofa and stayed there. I saw that my father owned a small television, and I moved as far from it as the sofa would permit.

My father, seeing this wasn't a brief visit, offered me supper. After we ate we went back to the living room and my father offered me a beer which I accepted. He didn't seem to know just how to get rid of me, and I chatted on about my job, oblivious of the time.

Finally—and I could see it took some effort—he suggested

that I stay the night. It was late, after all; I could drive home in the morning. So I thanked him and kept on talking.

One of my father's favorite subjects was local politics, so I had no difficulty setting him on that track. I let him have his head for awhile and then I mentioned a politician named David Hart. "Whatever became of him?" I asked.

"Oh, I don't know. He tried to make a comeback, but it failed. I think the public had lost faith in him."

I knew of course that Hart had been district attorney when the Count Electric murders had occurred and that it was Hart's failure to bring the killer to justice that had ruined his career. But I am a subtle man. "Lost faith?" I asked.

"He couldn't catch Count Electric, the serial murderer. He said he would and he didn't. Most folks saw it as a lie."

"I wonder what became of Count Electric," I said.

My father blinked at me. He seemed strangely agitated. He leaned forward, "Count Electric is dead," he said.

I laughed. "You say that with some conviction. Did you kill him?"

It was my imagination and the darkness of the room, no doubt, but my father seemed on the verge of saying something far different from what he in fact said. He said: "Most of the psychological studies suggest the man *must* have killed himself. These serial killers don't just retire. They keep at it until they are caught or until they unravel. I expect they just never matched up the suicide with the madman." My father paused, slapped his hands on his knees. "I'm going to bed. I'll get you some blankets for the sofa. You are free to come to church with me in the morning although I don't expect you'll care to. You and your mother were never churchgoers."

I said I thought I would sleep in late and my father nodded. Surprisingly, I didn't feel any disapproval in his nod.

I didn't sleep well, plagued by bad dreams. Once, getting out of bed to relieve my bladder, I stumbled, discovering that my left leg was without sensation. I hobbled to the bathroom and blinked at my reflection in the mirror. I was rapidly approaching forty, and the mirror, aided by a cruel fluorescent light, held an unflattering reflection. The left side of my face had stiffened somewhat under the advent of the migraine, and I looked querulous and thin-lipped and more than a little like my father.

I went back to the sofa and lay down but could not sleep. Bright swarming lights suggested that a bruising headache was on its way. I walked out into the backyard, saw the toolshed, and decided to investigate. This wasn't prudent, of course. But I needed some distraction, something to perhaps keep the migraine at bay.

I was looking for the suitcase my mother had written about. There was no great likelihood that it still existed, or that, if it did, it still contained the machine that had frightened her. Still . . .

The toolshed had not had time to acquire the organic clutter and rich moldiness that is a toolshed's natural destiny. It held an old canvas tarp, gardening tools, a shovel, mason jars of nails and bolts, a wheelbarrel. Under the bare electric bulb, I was able to ascertain, in less than five minutes, that the shed contained no suitcase.

I went back inside the house and drank a glass of water. The lights had subsided in my head, and I could feel my left foot. I felt oddly alert.

The kitchen was cozy, and I sat at the formica-topped table where we had eaten dinner. The gas stove and round-shouldered refrigerator were old but not in disrepair. They seemed cheerful, comfortable, far less intimidating than my own kitchen's modern appliances. I found myself envying my father's domesticity. Next to the refrigerator was a door. I opened it—it was warped and popped open with a waffling hum—and flicked a light. Stairs led down into a cellar of cinderblock walls and an earth floor.

I found the suitcase on a wooden shelf under a pile of old *National Geographics.* It was not locked and I opened it, prepared, as always, for disappointment. And there it was. I removed it carefully, with an odd sense of rescuing it from its confinement. I placed it on the bare floor and stood back.

After all these years, it gleamed, a thing of polished metal surfaces. I now understood my mother's inarticulateness in its presence. It suggested a steel spider or dog, veined with insulated wires. Needles gleamed at the ends of jointed appendages. I sat down and studied it at great length. It contained a number of leather straps, and as my mind adjusted to the machine, I realized that these straps would bind it to its victim.

I found myself grinning, wondering what, indeed, my mother must have made of this thing. A bundle of thick wires traveled down its spine and under its belly entering what was unmistakably a large silver dildo. Close inspection showed that this prosthetic penis was made of steel, machined and polished on a lathe. My father had owned just such a lathe.

An electrical cord protruded like a tail—it was impossible not to think in terms of an animal. A dial on the back and a number of switches suggested that current could be directed to various appendages and regulated as to voltage.

I have an analytical mind and a quick imagination. We were talking electrical rape here. Count Electric's reputation for perversity was, apparently, deserved. No wonder the newspapers were vague about the precise nature of death. I now recalled one newspaper speaking of "the unusual nature and location of burns resulting from high voltages." Unusual, indeed!

I was lost in contemplation of this strange machine, and did not immediately notice my father at the top of the stairs. I have no idea how long he had been standing there, but when I turned, he spoke my name.

"Mark," he said, "you have abused my hospitality."

I laughed. It was such a formal thing to say, under the circumstances.

"I'm sorry," I said. "Excuse me, Count."

Now he frowned. "Count?" He shook his head. "I am not the author of that machine. If you think that, your snooping has not rewarded you with the truth."

"Oh," I said. "Well, if you are not Count Electric, then who is?"

"Why you are, of course."

I blinked at him.

My father nodded slowly. "You don't remember. Count Electric is dead, and I should have destroyed his machine a long time ago. What possessed me to keep it? I have no idea." My father began to come down the stairs, stopped. "I waited for his return, always fearing his arrival. But he appeared to be gone for good. He had been cauterized in the accident. You were free of him. I couldn't bring any of those girls back. And you were—are—for all our differences, my son, my blood."

I did not know what he was talking about, although some clamoring thing inside me seemed to tear at the knowledge.

My father explained.

I had been living with them then, a morose stranger in their house. My father had seen me coming and going at all hours, but he had said nothing. He understood that I was, after all, twenty-two years old and if finances prevented me from finding a place of my own, they did not prevent me from living my own life.

One night he had been awakened by a scream. My mother continued to sleep, and my father went downstairs. He was almost convinced that the scream had been a product of dreams when he heard a curious buzzing noise which led him to the door to my room. The sound was coming from behind my door, and he could see, in the crack beneath the door, a flickering blue light. The door was locked, so my father ran outside, found the window to my room, broke it, and entered. The scene that greeted him was extraordinary. I seemed to lie in a blanket of blue light while being savaged by a ravenous creature made of steel. For a moment, he was paralyzed with fear. The oxygen had been leached from the air, replaced by coppery smoke. My father found the cord, yanked it from the wall, and the blue light vanished; the steel beast crumpled on its side. My father called an ambulance, returned to my room and, sensing the diabolical nature of the machine, shoved it in a closet. Realizing that some source for the shock would be required, he poured lighter fluid over my television and set it on fire.

I was in the hospital a long time. While I was there, my father made a close inspection of the machine that left no doubt in his mind as to its function. He searched my room with great thoroughness, and he discovered the newspaper clippings taped to the back of the dresser's mirror. He resolved to go to the police. He would not have any young woman's death on his conscience.

No doubt I had been initiating some refinement or repair on the machine when it had shorted out and—you might say—turned on me.

All of this, of course, he kept from my mother.

But he hesitated. I returned to the house and he watched

me. I healed slowly. I had to relearn the most rudimentary of things. And whole areas were lost to me forever. I had been, for instance, a piano player of some skill. Now I was unable to play a note and the problem was not simply one of impaired dexterity. Music itself, its logic, eluded me. I had lost that particular talent.

And as my father watched my recovery, a hope began to grow. It seemed that the accident had killed the monstrosity within me. Count Electric was dead. And my father said nothing.

3

We talked a great deal that night. I was stunned by this new knowledge. To think that I had once been such a monster. What had inspired this pathology? My parents were normal enough. I was unaware of any deep hatred of women—although I confess to a conviction that there is no pleasing them. I have always been fascinated by sex, but impotent through a deep sense of fear and inadequacy. Perhaps potency was all I craved—and I sought it in a misguided, socially inexcusable fashion.

A curious excitement overtook me. I tried to present a suitably dismayed exterior, but I found myself experiencing a furtive delight.

In the morning, my father left for church. I suspect he had more than the usual amount of praying to do. My knowing could alter things. Perhaps I would find a renewed and unhealthy interest in Count Electric. What would he do?

I didn't really think my father would do anything—at least not right away. But since a new life was presenting itself to me, I thought I should sever connections with the old.

My father had installed a garbage disposal under the sink. It was capable of generating considerable voltage. I imagined a man with his hands up to his elbows in soapy water suddenly triggering all those volts. What would the trigger be? A time factor perhaps. The water itself, the pressure. A water-sensitive switch?

The cellar was a fruitful source of electrical parts. While what I finally contrived was not elegant, it would certainly work. There were already dirty dishes in the sink and my father was a man who liked things clean and in their place.

I left him a note saying I needed some time alone and that I was taking the horrid machine with me. I was going to dismantle it and throw its pieces in the Potomac, I wrote. I went down to the cellar and packed it in its suitcase.

4

Elizabeth was a great consolation during the funeral. She said that it must have been particularly devastating—my finding the body. I agreed.

I had driven back to Waterford the next day, after dialing my father's number several times and listening to the phone ring.

My father lay in the middle of the kitchen with his sleeves rolled up and his eyes open. His expression was blank and in no way accusatory. A fuse had blown and after restoring the garbage disposal to a more conventional mode, I went down in the basement, found the fusebox and replaced the blown fuse. Back in the kitchen, I finished washing the dishes—knowing my father would approve—and then called the police. There was no question of foul play. My father was an old man with a weak heart.

"You've suffered so much," Elizabeth said, rubbing my

neck. "You need to get away for awhile. We could go somewhere. Just the two of us."

I have, of course, reflected long and hard on the origin of
Count Electric. Whatever could have made me assume such
a bizarre personality? Was I traumatized as a child, driven
from the path of virtue by poor parenting? Was I the victim
of a raging inner child? Did an overly critical teacher kick
me over the edge?

Well, it is no fair looking for Freudian excuses in a troubled
past. I've always felt that was cheating. I suspect that what
we have here is simple Evil, nothing more, no apologies
forthcoming.

The machine's short was easy to discover and repair. I
saw quickly how the machine was used, how the various
appendages could deliver small shocks, create a series of almost orgasmic convulsions in the victim. And, of course,
the coup de grâce would be reserved for the artificial penis.
There was a certain artistry involved . . .

Elizabeth fondles me constantly when we are together.
Poor girl, she can't know how this demeans me.

I have agreed to go away with her for a brief vacation. I
have urged her to tell no one, and she has agreed. I have
already reserved a motel room in North Carolina. I have
used Elizabeth's name for the reservation.

Yes, I suppose I am Evil. Odd that it seems so much less
than that. I am excited of course—but it is the excitement of
the scientist, really. It is the sense of discovery, of uncharted
worlds, that drives me on. Will the machine still work?

5

Elizabeth was all giggles. Although we were both grown-
ups, there was a sneaky, adolescent feel to the whole busi-

ness. She came back to the car with the keys and winked at me.

"Too late to turn back now," she said.

"No turning back," I agreed.

I drove around to our room on the far end of the "L." We had arrived late at night, for I had insisted on working that morning. Elizabeth ran from the car and opened the motel door. I followed her in.

Elizabeth turned and looked at me. She was not a beautiful woman, with a nose that was slightly too long and a sort of desperate, old-maidish enthusiasm. But she looked quite lovely, welcoming me. She giggled, my electric bride.

"Is that the best you can do for luggage?" she said.

I looked down at the cheap, battered suitcase. Mildew spotted it, and my best efforts had been unable to erase some brown stains.

I smiled back. "Well," I said, "it has sentimental value."

Graven Images

"Well, what have we got today?" the man said, seating himself in the chair, his back to the window so that he was silhouetted against the twilight.

"Back already?" Benny said. One of the things Benny hated about the man was his heartiness, the slick, salesman's boom of his voice. "I thought I had seen the last of you for awhile."

"I can leave if you'd like," the man said. He had the blackmailer's upper hand, and he knew it.

"Okay, okay," Benny said, reaching over to the nightstand and opening the drawer. He took the photographs out and spread them on the bed.

The man leaned forward. "We could use some more light," he said.

Benny walked to the door and flipped a switch. The room brightened, and he walked back as the man lifted one of the photographs and held it up.

"Tell me about this one," the man said.

Benny took the photo and sat on the edge of the bed. His shoulders sagged. "Well, that's my daughter Lucy. She was nine years old or thereabouts. And in the wagon is our dog, Zenith. She would haul that dog all over town, dress him up, go rolling down a hill with him clutched to her chest. Zenith doted on Lucy and so he let her do most anything. I guess men and dogs are alike in that respect. They'll tolerate some rough handling from the women they love."

"The house in the background," the man said. "Yours?"

"Well, we lived there. That's on Cedar Avenue. We rented it for three years in the early fifties. Our landlord lived next door, an old Italian man who didn't speak much English and always wore a suit. They sold the house shortly after he hanged himself, so we had to move. I remember it was his brother who came to our door and told us the news. I didn't know who he was. There was this small, tearful man in suspenders standing at my door. He was wearing a white shirt with the sleeves rolled up, and he looked real frail, and the first words he spoke were: 'My brother he is suicided with the chair.' And I didn't know what he was talking about or who he was, but Eileen came up behind me—she always saw straight to a person's heart—and walked quick past me and took him in her arms and he went to sobbing on her shoulder while she held him."

Benny sighed. "She was good with people, Eileen."

"I'll take it," the man said, standing up.

Benny blinked. "What?"

"The photo. This one will do," the man said.

That was in the summer—at Brodin Memorial Hospital. In November, Benny woke in his own home in the middle of the night to relieve his bladder, and he heard a sound in the kitchen.

It was the man again, seated at the kitchen table. He had poured himself a glass of milk.

"Just make yourself at home," Benny said.

The man smiled broadly. "Oh, I'm comfortable most anywhere," the man said.

"I bet," Benny said. He knew why the man had come.

Without saying a word, he left the kitchen and returned with the photographs. He tossed them on the kitchen table.

The man finished his glass of milk, and tapped one of the photos.

"That's Lucy graduating from high school," Benny said. "What's to say? The day was hot, I remember that. She's wearing a bathing suit under that black gown. So were a lot of the kids. They went . . . look, you want it, you got it." Benny handed the photo to the man.

"They went to the beach," the man said.

"Yeah." Benny stood up. "You got your photo. It's two in the morning, and I'm going back to bed. You know the way out."

The man shook his head. "No. I'm not interested in that one. This one, perhaps. That's your wife, isn't it? And the young man, who's he?"

"That's Danny Miller. He played clarinet in a band. And that's Eileen, all right. She wasn't my wife then. Hey, maybe you want this picture. It's yours."

"I'll take it," the man said.

"You son of a bitch."

"Well, I'm not a fool. She looks quite luminous in this picture, breathless, and the lights in her hair . . . you kissed her for the first time that night, or I can't read a photo."

"Take it and get out," Benny said.

As the man walked toward the door, Benny shouted at his back: "I don't need a photograph to call up that night. There ain't so goddam many perfect moments in a man's life that they get clouded with time. Ask me what perfume she wore. Ask me what the band played or how the champagne tasted or what the night air felt like or how the back of her neck surprised my hand that first time I kissed her."

The man didn't turn around. He walked down the hall and out the door without a word.

A year later, the week before Christmas, Benny was watching the rain fall, a grim, flat attack on the hospital's parking lot. The man came up behind him.

"You gave me a start," Benny said.

The man apologized. He seemed to have put on weight since Benny had last seen him. He seemed, in fact, tired, disheartened.

"Well," Benny said. "Here's what I've got."

This time the man sat on the bed next to Benny, and Benny showed him the photographs.

"This is Aunt Kate," Benny said. "She made the best fudge brownies. And she loved to sing. She would sing 'Amazing Grace' while washing the dishes."

"No," the man said. He was shaking his head. He stood up and thumbed through the photos in his hands. "You insult me. These are not the goods. These are not . . . these are not your photographs."

Benny chuckled. "You are sharp. I got to give you that, you are sharp."

The man threw the photos on the floor. "In all our dealings, we have been above board. I am disappointed in you."

"Those are Lou Himmel's photographs. Perhaps you recognized them. That really is Aunt Kate. Lou's Aunt Kate, not mine. Lou being dead, I figured he wouldn't mind."

"I wish to see your photographs."

Benny shrugged. "I burned them."

"You know what this means."

Now Benny stood up. "Yeah, it means I don't give a goddam. Now get out of here."

The man sighed and looked around the room as though

seeking a reasonable audience. "I'll complete the paperwork, then."

"Whatever lights your fire," Benny said. "Whatever honks your horn."

The storm raged outside. Benny was watching the six o'clock news when Nurse Cable—everyone on the ward called her Julie—entered. She was a pretty young woman with black hair, cut rather severely, and a lush Georgia accent. She took Benny's blood pressure. "How are you doing?" she asked.

"Poorly," Benny said. "I'm an old man, and anyone my age who says he is feeling great has simply forgotten what it means to feel great. I'm going to die, you know."

"Oh, I don't think so. These tests are perfectly routine. We all die someday, but I don't think you'll die today, Mr. Levin."

"Oh, I don't mind," Benny said. "I'm sick of the game, frankly. What sort of a game is it when your opponent can look at the cards when he deals the hands? I'm beginning to think that Lucy had the best of it."

"Lucy?"

"My daughter."

"I didn't know you had a daughter."

"I did. She drowned."

"I'm sorry."

"Well, that's the point, isn't it? We are all sorry for what's inevitable. Piece by piece it is taken away from us. We appear to bargain, but it all comes to the same thing in the end. Death and condolences."

Julie fluffed the old man's pillow. "You are in a morbid frame of mind tonight, Mr. Levin, I'll say that. I'm not sure I can absorb so much philosophy this evening. There are

79

three very sick people on the ward, and some less sick ones that need a bit of coddling."

Benny chuckled. "That's the spirit. Youth has no business mucking with philosophy and despair."

"Not during work hours anyway," Julie said. She left.

It was nearly ten when she returned. Benny was sitting up in bed looking at a photograph.

"He missed this one," Benny said. "He held it right in his hand, but he thought it was one of Lou's."

"I'm afraid I don't understand," Julie said. She had to go. There were meds to disperse, I.V.'s to regulate.

He handed the photo to her. "It doesn't look like much, I suppose."

It didn't. The photo was black and white, and showed a motel looking like a grey shoe box on its side. There were some vague mountains in the background hoarding rain clouds, and you could almost hear the hiss of tires on a wet highway. A sign said: Parkway Motel. The camera, a cheap box-camera judging by the quality of the image, had been jarred during the exposure, tilting and blurring everything.

"Eileen hugged me just as I snapped it," Benny said. Benny laughed and took the photo back. "Oh, I don't expect you to admire the beauty of the photo. Its charms are all internal. That was our honeymoon. We stayed there the first day on our way down to Key West."

Julie said she had been to Key West a year ago with her parents, and the conversation turned to the despicable nature of land developers and the apathy of the powerful. Than Julie had to get back to work.

Benny watched the eleven o'clock news that evening and then turned the TV off and went into the bathroom. He turned the shower on, brushed his teeth.

When Benny turned back to the shower, the man was standing under the fall of water, his dark suit soaked, his hair plastered against his forehead, his small eyes grim and veiled by the twin waterfalls pouring over the bony ridge of his brow.

"Son of a bitch!" Benny said, stepping backward as though bitten. He slipped then, reached out for a handhold, and caught only a draped towel that came away from its rung, falling with him. The back of his head slammed against the tiled floor.

"Are you all right?" Eileen asked. Her face was inches from his. The shower was still on, the pouring water making a mist behind her head.

"I slipped," Benny said. "Wow." Eileen helped him up, an arm around his waist. She was still fully dressed, a dark dress with white dots, and she was soaked. Benny was suddenly aware of his nakedness. He had never been naked with Eileen, and he felt awkward and ungainly. The throb at the back of his head was insignificant.

Eileen dried him and hustled him under the covers. "Are you okay?" she asked, leaning over him.

"I'm fine," he said, reaching to touch her cheek. "But you are soaked."

"That's easily remedied," his new bride said, and she shucked her dress in one effortless motion, the wet garment rising over her head, her slip following. She walked toward him, glowing, her crooked smile enriched by the fullness of her hips.

"I wish I had a photograph of you right now," Benny said.

"Not on your life, fellow," she said, crawling under the covers. "You'll have to settle for a snapshot of this motel."

And the shock of her body, its full length falling upon him, clicked the shutter of his heart.

Pep Talk

Nadine's note was on the refrigerator, and I read it and said, out loud, "There goes my heart."

That was the beginning, I guess, the first time I talked to myself ever. My mother had always maintained that talking to oneself was a sign of mental decline, and it was certainly true that uncle Walt, who talked to himself constantly, seemed to confirm this belief. At any rate, Floppy, our dog, was in the kitchen, and maybe I was talking to him, although the truth is I had never confided much in him and didn't think of him as a sympathetic ear.

Nadine's note was short and written in the flowery script she'd learned going to a night class. It said, "Roger, I have left you and I will come by and get Floppy and my things on Saturday. Do not—I repeat—do not call me at the office.

"I am sorry it had to end this way, but there wasn't any future for us. It is nobody's fault, but we were not compatible people. I hope you have a good life and when you are very old can look back on it with no regrets. Always your friend, Nadine."

I opened the refrigerator door and, on a whim, opened the freezer compartment and stuck my head in. "Nadine," I whispered, "You have broke my heart."

Nadine came by on Saturday, accompanied by her girlfriend Emily. Nadine is not a beautiful girl, mostly thanks to an expression of disgust that is her constant companion, but Nadine is a knock-out compared to Emily, who is stout with a vicious smile and a way of rocking back on her heels while she gives you the once-over that is unsettling.

"Hey Roger, how you doing?" Emily said.

I didn't say anything. I went into the bedroom and shut the door and lay there on the bed, watching the ceiling fan go around. A ceiling fan can be a blur, or you can try to hang onto one of the blades with your eyes and let it swing you around. This last is a queasy business and I abandoned it after a half hour. When I came back out, Nadine went into the bedroom and got her clothes. "You are not being much help," Nadine said when she walked back past me with an armload of dresses.

"I'm doing my best," I said.

After Nadine and Emily left, taking Floppy with them, I said, "It's just you and me, Roger."

And that's when I started talking to myself in earnest. It wasn't a gradual process. "What will you have for breakfast?" I asked myself, and I said, "Some Cheerios, I guess."

"Bananas?"

"No thanks."

"You sure?" I guess what hooked me on talking to myself was the concern in my voice. You can't get that from strangers—or even most friends.

I spent the weekend by myself and when I got to the office on Monday, I found I didn't have much to say. Ordinarily I might have told Arlene, our bookkeeper, about Nadine's leaving, and at lunch I might have asked Howard Peters his opinion of the situation. But I found I wasn't interested in talking to anyone. I was waiting until I got home and could talk to myself.

I noticed, in the next few weeks, that talking to myself was more interesting than I would have thought.

Sometimes I would treat myself as though I were a dim-witted child. "You better take an umbrella," I would tell myself. "It's raining."

"Well, I know that," I would say. I would sound exasperated, but I wasn't really. I liked being worried over.

Most of the time I didn't have long, windy conversations with myself. I'm not, after all, deranged. It was more like I would pass myself in the hall and exchange a few words. "Another dreaded day, another dismal dollar," I would say.

I would laugh, nod, and say, "Life is hell."

If you start talking to yourself day in and day out, you will find that you don't want brilliance; you just want something comfortable like the talk of old married couples, just something to bounce off the walls, something to navigate by.

Nadine had taken the TV. The radio she had left only pulled in one station, a station dominated by what sounded like a bedridden evangelist who thumbed through the Bible and read whatever struck his fancy. I had a very clear picture of this evangelist as a fat, pale man in a bathrobe, his chins quivering as he spoke. I imagined that his children refused to talk to him. I sympathized with his situation, but I couldn't listen to his show. So my apartment would have been pretty quiet if I hadn't taken to talking to myself.

Often I would address myself in a polite but distant manner. There's a lot to be said for politeness and common decency.

"Want another cup of coffee?" I would ask.

"No thank you, really," I'd say.

Every week or so that summer Nadine would call to see how I was doing. We had been living together for three years before she left, and she thought of herself as an authority on me. She said she was concerned, because I wasn't one to get out and do things. She was afraid I would slide into a depression.

Somewhere in September, she stopped calling me. Our last conversation had ended badly. That was when she said she thought she might be bisexual.

"What?" I said.

"Emily thinks I might be bisexual," Nadine said.

"Ha!" I said. "Emily!"

"What do you mean by that?" Nadine wanted to know. I knew that tone in her voice, and I knew better than to speak my mind candidly when that tone appeared, but I did it anyway.

"Well," I said. "A mouse shouldn't, just generally speaking, put too much stock in the opinions of a cat."

Nadine chunked the phone down on that sentence, and I was rewarded with a loud dial tone.

"Bit of a huff? Small snit, your Highness?" I delivered the lines in a thin, British-by-way-of-Monty Python, accent. I liked the effect.

In the weeks that followed, I found I could enliven my conversations with myself by adopting a variety of voices and accents. These developed into characters, some of whom were particularly helpful in certain circumstances. For instance, a down-home drawl was a great comfort when I was embarked on a home repair project. Having ripped the threads from a piece of rusted pipe while attempting to unclog the sink, it helped immeasurably to have a slow, cozy voice say, "Well, Roger old boy, I reckon you have made a gawd-awful mess of it."

I'd shrug my shoulder. "I guess so."

"Hell, even the best coon dog loses the scent sometimes. Let's call us a time out here. Have a beer."

"I suppose so," I would say, not anywhere near as reluctant as I sounded, and feeling much calmer already.

In November, my birthday rolled around and Nadine—
who, I've got to admit, wasn't a woman to hold a grudge—
called. "Happy birthday!" she said. "How does it feel to be
thirty?"

"Not bad."

"Do you have company? Oh, they're singing 'Happy
Birthday,' aren't they? Friends from the office?"

"Not exactly. Look, I better go."

"Sure. I didn't mean to interrupt. Happy birthday, Roger.
Happy birthday."

I hung up and cut myself another piece of cake. I had spent
the whole morning blowing up balloons, and my chest hurt
some, but I was happy. I rewound the tape and played it again.

"Happy Birthday dear Rogeeeer, Happy—"

I had bought a tape recorder for positive affirmations. A
positive affirmation—in case you have missed the last couple
of decades—is like when you go up to a mirror and say, "I
love you, Roger." This sort of thing improves your self-
image and just naturally dispels negativity. I had tried it but
I hadn't had much luck with it.

"I love you, Roger."

"Well thank you," I'd say, but I would feel awkward, and
at a disadvantage, like I wasn't responding enthusiastically
enough. Actually, if I were someone else, I wouldn't want
to hug me. I'm not that kind of guy. I might shake my hand,
but I wouldn't hug me. And I would appreciate not being
hugged.

Anyway, I bought this little tape recorder at K-Mart and
read the instructions and spoke into it, "You are a warm and
loving person, Roger."

When I played it back, I was a little disappointed. I didn't
sound like a person I could trust. And I sure didn't sound
warm. I sounded smug, like some sort of con artist that has
just pulled a fast one.

I worked at it, consciously deepening my voice. If I rolled up a magazine and used it like a megaphone, that seemed to help. The trick was to be positive without being hearty. I wanted to be comforted, not slapped on the back.

"You are getting better every day in every way," I crooned, sitting cross-legged on the floor and megaphoning my voice toward the microphone on the carpet. "The world is your oyster, Roger Gilroy."

Of course, I eventually came to the conclusion that I would get better results if I had better equipment. "Love yourself enough to buy the best," I advised myself.

So I bought this elaborate tape recorder that had four tracks. You could "mix-down" on it—I think that's how the salesman put it—so that I could record my voice on top of my voice. I could do it over and over again and sound like a whole chorus of me's.

Well, I didn't master it overnight, but I was pretty good at it by the time my birthday rolled around, and that, of course, is what Nadine had heard.

Anyone will tell you that the more you get into a hobby, the more it takes on a life of its own. Pretty soon I had acquired eight cheap tape recorders to supplement the fancy one. And then I discovered electronic timing devices. I'm no electronics whiz, but the trick of mastering anything is perseverance. You'd be amazed at what you can do if you hang in there.

When I came home at night and turned the light switch on, a chorus of voices would greet me. "Hey, Rog. How you doing?"

"Long day?"

"Grab a beer boy."

"You look beat. You're working too hard."

I almost forgot about Christmas. But Nadine reminded

me by showing up on my doorstep. There she was when I opened the door.

It was a cold winter, and she was dressed for it. She had on one of those red and white knit caps and a yellow woolen scarf and her famous over-fed grizzly coat.

"Nadine," I said.

"Yep," she said, "I got you a present. Merry Christmas."

She walked on in and I closed the door behind her. I was wearing a raincoat, which I'd tossed on over my underwear in order to answer the door.

Nadine sat on the sofa. "You are wearing a raincoat," she said. She was never one to miss anything.

"Well yeah. I didn't know who might be at the door."

Nadine nodded. "Open your present," she said, looking around the room as she shrugged out of her coat. She was wearing a sweatshirt promoting a rock band called "Carload of Feminists."

I started peeling off the gift wrap (cats in Santa suits).

"Who's our most favorite person? Roger Gilroy! Who! Roger Gilroy. I can't hear you! Rooooooooger Gilroy!"

"What's that?" Nadine asked, already standing.

Cheers and whistles were coming from the bathroom. I looked at my watch.

"That's the eleven o'clock pick-me-up cheer."

I put my hands on Nadine's shoulders and eased her back onto the sofa. The cheer was subsiding.

"It's nothing," I assured her as I went back to unwrapping her gift. "Hey this is great."

It was a book entitled, *Your Best Self: How to Grow into Your Potential.* The author's photo on the back showed a slightly overweight man wearing sunglasses and grinning broadly as he stepped off a yacht.

Nadine leaned forward. "I thought this book might really turn your life around. I mean, it has done wonders for me."

I went over and hugged her, an affectionate, ex-lover hug. "Well, I can use all the help I can get. I'm sorry I didn't get you anything. I forgot all about Christmas."

"I'm not so crazy about Christmas myself," Nadine said, sagging a little. "It's been difficult. Lydia is moving out."

I didn't know anybody named Lydia, so of course I asked who Lydia was and I got the whole story. Lydia was a performance artist and a lesbian, and she and Nadine had become lovers. Emily had warned right from the start that it wouldn't work, but Nadine hadn't listened.

I sympathized. I said how human relationships were difficult, how it was hard to keep the lines of communication open, et cetera.

"And you?" Nadine asked. "How are you doing, really?" She wiped her eyes. She is a woman who should cry in private, since weeping actually seems to elongate her nose somehow, and red blotches appear on her cheeks.

"I'm doing okay," I said. "I'm adjusting."

"Are you dating anyone?" Nadine asked.

"Well . . ." I paused. "I guess I'm just working on myself these days."

"That's probably what I should be doing," Nadine said. She put her coat back on, struggling a little but managing.

"See you," I said as she marched down the walk. I don't think she heard me, and as it was cold, I shut the door before she reached her car.

I looked at my watch. It was almost noon. I was glad she had left before the Lunchtime Affirmation. That's a very loud bit, including some drum-like noises I created with a cardboard box and some harmonica sounds that I've really labored over. I'm still not one hundred percent pleased with it, but it's getting there.

Looking Out For Eleanor

LOU

The gas station attendant's name was Walter Reed, and I said I had been in a hospital with that name once, and he said, "What for?" and I said, "Malaria," and he nodded his head as though he knew all about it. He stared past me through the window, and I turned, and we both watched Ellie get out of the car. Walter Reed squinted the way a farmer will study a perfectly clear sky, skeptical-like. Ellie does, I got to say, look too good to be true.

She was wearing faded jeans, scuffed boots, and one of my old work shirts. She was smiling as she approached us, moving with her farm-girl grace, her curly brown hair dancing like a swarm of bees. The heater on the car was out, and it had been cold last night, coming east. Now the morning sun was blazing, and if you stayed out of the wind, it was warm. Ellie always was a warm weather girl, and she'd been singing along with the radio all morning, in such high spirits that I hesitated to stop. But the gauge was reading empty, and there wasn't any way around it.

"Your wife?" Walter Reed asked. He had his elbows on the counter. He turned and looked up at me with a sly smile—as though a good looking woman was a joke we shared.

"That's Ellie," I said. Then, like a fool, I said, "Don't say anything to her. It would be best if you don't even look at her."

That did it, of course. "I reckon I'll look at who I please and speak if I've a mind to," he said, turning away from me. "It's a free country."

Then Ellie swung the screen door open and brought all her energy into the store. It wasn't a big room, and I felt the oxygen burning out of it, and I had a vision of a lot of plastic bags full of corn chips and pretzels exploding under pressure.

"I need a Coke and a couple of Snickers," she said to me. She was heading off down the candy aisle when Walter Reed spoke to her, to her back actually cause she had flown by him like he was invisible. He said, "Hi Ellie."

She spun around as though he'd caught her by the shoulder.

"Excuse me?" She was still smiling. She clutched her brown leather purse against her stomach, rocked back on her heels and shot me a quick glance.

"Lou. He just said my name. I don't know him. Honest, I don't."

"It's all right." I was speaking fast, feeling blood beat in my throat. "He don't know the situation."

A fool could have heard the warning in my voice, but not that gas station attendant. He opened his mouth and said, "Maybe we met somewheres and it slipped your mind, Ellie, and—"

I got scared. For a moment, I saw the truck driver again, lying in the dirt with his wide, white belly showing under the t-shirt, his arms flung out like a drunken evangelist, blood all over his throat from where the bullet had shut him up in mid-sentence.

Ellie was still smiling, but that was just because she'd forgot to stop. Her eyes told the whole story, and I figured I had about thirty seconds. I had my knife out, hooked the blade out with my thumb, and was around the counter in ten.

I caught the hair on the back of Walter Reed's head—it was long and brown and felt dirty—and banged his forehead against the counter. His cap flew off, and he shouted something. He tried to turn, and I gave him a quick cut on his cheek just to show I was sincere and said, "Don't move at all," and he stiffened like a bird dog on point. I looked up and shouted at Ellie. "It's all right," I shouted. "This is under control, here. This ain't no big deal."

Ellie just stood there.

Walter Reed was one of those skinny guys that surprise you with their strength, and he made a sudden turn—like a trout that comes alive in your hands—and threw me back against the soda machine and scrambled for something under the counter. I ducked low and when he turned with the gun I head-butted him in the gut and that was the fight; he folded. Like a lot of skinny guys, he had a weak stomach.

I grabbed up the revolver and stuffed it in the pocket of my windbreaker, snapped the knife shut, and said, without looking behind me, "Get on in the car, Ellie."

Ellie turned and ran out the door. Walter Reed was moaning now. He'd rolled over on his stomach and got up on his knees.

"Look," I said, "It's too bad. I told you not to say anything. I'm looking out for her, see. It's a complicated business . . ." My words just ran out, and I thought: *I ain't gonna explain it*—not to this Walter Reed fellow and not to the cops he's gonna call as soon as I'm out of here.

So I took the revolver out and shot him behind the ear. I just felt sick, doing it, but I took a few deep breaths, braced against the counter, and said, out loud, "It's a cold, old world, Lou." I put the gun back in my pocket and emptied the register. I'm no thief, but the money wasn't doing Walter any good.

I went back to the car. Ellie was sitting on the passenger's side, staring straight ahead.

"Look," I said, "I got you them Snickers. And a Coke."

She smiled like the sun coming up on the Fourth of July. It done me good, that smile.

MALCOLM

I don't like to lecture, and I was somewhat dismayed to hear the note of admonishment that entered my voice when Mrs. Hamilton said, "You're sweet on that Eleanor Greer."

Mrs. Hamilton has been working for Taylor County Department of Social Services for thirty-two years, almost as long as I have been alive, and time has eroded—assuming, of course, that such ever existed—her professional bearing. She treats her clients as though they were errant children, insists on calling them by their first names, fills out their forms for them, and gives them advice for circumventing policies that she dismisses as being "bureaucratic bullshit." She seems to understand nothing of the boundaries that are required of a social worker.

I have been with the agency seven years myself, and I see quite clearly what has happened to Mrs. Hamilton: She has "gone native." She has chosen, it seems to me, to abandon her professional ethics for a kind of chumminess, a camaraderie with the disenfranchised. Perhaps she has despaired, and this is the result. I suppose it may happen to me with time. But it hasn't happened yet. I still believe in conducting myself in a professional manner and in maintaining the proper distance in my dealings with clients.

I wear a suit, and I don't, like Bradford or Daugherty, loosen my tie, roll up my sleeves, and affect a harried, hungover air. I strive for a well-groomed, neat appearance, despite the failings of municipal air conditioning during the long Texas summers.

"I can tell you are sweet on that Eleanor Greer," Mrs. Hamilton said.

"Mrs. Hamilton," I replied, "I am not sweet on Eleanor Greer. Miss Greer is a client, a recipient of our services, and my interest in her is one of professional concern. I realize that you are speaking in jest, but I find the suggestion insulting. Not only is Miss Greer in need of financial help, she is also, as you know, developmentally disabled. To suggest that I would harbor romantic feelings for a woman who is, mentally and emotionally, a child is to suggest that I am a child molester."

I had overstated the case, of course. Eleanor didn't score high on intelligence tests, and her emotional responses were not always in context, but she was not impaired in any clinical sense. Mrs. Hamilton was, in any event, undaunted.

"She doesn't look too developmentally deprived to me," Mrs. Hamilton said, looking at me over the tops of her glasses. Mrs. Hamilton often resembled a dissolute Einstein, had that great scientist gained fifty pounds and taken a fancy to wearing polka-dot dresses. She continued: "And I believe I have seen your eyes assessing her developments with approval. You can say what you want, Malcolm Blair, that woman turns you on. I don't see you rushing to get coffee for Mrs. Geller or old lady Barnes when they come in here."

I refused to respond. Silence is often the best defense.

I thought about what Mrs. Hamilton had said. I did look forward to seeing Eleanor Greer. She was a relief from the parade of petty criminals, alcoholics, schizophrenics and pathological liars that occupied most of my time.

I wasn't "sweet" on Eleanor Greer, but Mrs. Hamilton had, inadvertently, hit on the precise word to describe Eleanor. Aside from her extraordinary beauty, which lit up the shabby office, she had an innocence that was joyously feminine, a vulnerability that made me want to go the extra mile for her. My profession is inclined to make one cynical, and I welcomed Eleanor's visits as a soldier must welcome news of a victory during a long, grim war. She was so sweet-natured, so cheerful.

I was worried that I hadn't heard from her in two weeks. She was living with her brother and his wife, on a farm several miles outside of town. I went to her file and found her brother's telephone number and wrote it down. But then I changed my mind and decided a country outing would do me good.

The drive out was over an ill-repaired, narrow road through generic Texas landscape, lots of scrub pine and twisted live oaks, their waxy leaves sprayed with fly-blown light—just a long, flat, relentless vista in which prickly pear cactus dotted the land like floral acne.

I missed the turn-off, got lost, and had to ask at a roadside grocery, where a black dog came out from behind a bin of lettuce and sniffed my crotch while making a low growling noise. "Don't mind Horace," the obese woman behind the counter told me. She glared at the dog, who ignored her. "He knows I'll beat him senseless iffen he bites one more customer."

Reassured, I asked directions and was told that I had just passed Mosely (the road I sought). I bought a Milky Way—my lunch—and left.

A grey cat, anorexically thin, slid under the porch as I approached the house. I had my first twinge of misgiving. There was a good chance my visit would not be viewed with delight, and there was always, in my line of work, the possibility of violence. My co-worker Bob Daugherty had once been forced—by a drunken man brandishing a shotgun—to attempt the repair of an ancient television. Fortunately, Daugherty's antagonist had passed out, and tragedy had been averted. But it was the sort of thing that did happen in my business, so I was having reservations when I knocked on the door.

An unshaven, gaunt man in overalls appeared. I told him who I was and asked if Eleanor Greer was in.

"She ain't here," he told me. His hair stuck out oddly, as though he'd just arisen from bed.

I asked if he were Eleanor's brother Hank, and he nodded.

"Who is it?" someone shouted from behind him.

"It's that welfare fellow," Greer shouted back into the room. "I told him Eleanor ain't here."

A woman I took to be Hank Greer's wife appeared at his shoulder. "Hey," she said. "Ellie ain't here."

"Do you know when she'll be back?"

"You got a warrant?" the woman asked. She had short, blond hair and was pretty in a pinched, anxious way.

Her husband said, "Louise, go watch your soaps." He stepped out on the porch, pulling the door behind him before his wife could say another word. He drained the last of a beer and threw the empty can into the yard's tall grass.

He swayed a little, standing on the porch, and I realized the man was drunk.

"Look here, counselor," he said, turning to me, "She's gone."

"You don't know where she is?"

He studied me with disgust. "Ain't that what I just told you?" Suddenly he zipped down his fly, turned away from me, and urinated heavily into the grass. "I'm her own brother," he said, re-zipping his fly, "and I don't know where she is."

He turned back to me. "Come on." He clumped down the porch steps, and I followed him. We walked out into the backyard, past a rusting Toronado up on cinderblocks, and he stopped in front of a charred mattress lying in the weeds.

"They dragged it into the backyard, and they set it on fire. You tell me?" He rocked back on his boot heels, hands in his pockets.

We both stood looking at the burned mattress.

"Lou Willis is a crazy sonofabitch. He was crazy back in high school, and he ain't improved since. You don't want to go looking for Ellie, counselor. She's bound for hell, with my old buddy, Lou Willis."

"I'm afraid I don't understand," I said.

Hank shrugged. "What's to understand? They burned her bed and then they run off."

I walked around the bed. It had rained since the fire, and the mattress was a sodden loaf of ashes. When I knelt down and touched it, my fingers came away black.

Hank Greer spoke behind me. He'd leaned over and the loudness of his voice startled me.

"Looking for clues, counselor?" he asked.

LOU

I'm no Vietnam vet. I don't claim it. I got no right to it. I wasn't there any time when I caught the fever and had to come back. I didn't see action, and I don't pretend I did. But I did see the jungle, and it made an impression on me. I was born in west Texas, so before I went to Vietnam, I didn't know how green a land could be. I'd seen jungles on TV and in the movies, but TV isn't something that happens to a person; it's just a lot of pictures. You come from a hard, held-in place, wildness can throw you for a loop. I caught a kind of fever that wouldn't let go—so the army gave me a medical discharge. After Nam, Texas just seemed dried up— literally. I drank gallons of water. At night I'd hear a chopper roaring overhead, on its way to the local military base, and I'd break out in a sweat. I drove into Dallas and found a greenhouse and loaded up on big, tropical plants with waxy, catcher's mitt leaves. My mother, a thin, fierce-believing Baptist who wouldn't have cut Jesus any slack, would come into my room and eye those plants and frown and say, "I guess you have lost your mind." And I guess I had.

But I got by. You get used to anything. I got some training in air conditioning repair on Uncle Sam's tab, and I started working at Sloan Air Conditioning and Heating, and I met this girl, Marlene Summers, and we got married, and we got us a house, and I guess I looked as normal as a citizen of Texas can, until I seen her in the pickup with Lenny Sawyer and then I got depressed, but I didn't let on. I was thinking I would pull out of it. But I didn't. Marlene asked for a divorce, and moved to Waco. And I guess that would have finished me; I guess I would have smoked myself. Why play it to the last card? But I thought I'd go see Hank—we'd been in high school together—and I done that, and he was sort of a letdown, but that's where I met Ellie. The last time I'd seen Ellie Greer, she was just a shrimp, Hank's skinny kid sister. I was shocked at how she'd come along—almost em- barrassed, like she'd had an accident that no one talked about. She was as wild and natural as the jungle itself, and when she laughed I could hear the way the rain used to sound all silvery in the trees and I thought: *Goddam but I've been thirsty. And didn't even know it!*

I was shaken up after the gas station business, but I calmed down once we got on the Interstate. Ellie dozed off, just closed her eyes and leaned back and was gone, easy as a child. I studied her out of the corner of my eye and thought, "Lou Willis, you keep this woman from harm."

By the time Ellie woke up, I had thought things over. "How would you like to go to Florida?" I asked her.

"I never been," she said, and laughed. "I don't know about Florida."

"We could go see my daddy down in St. Petersburg. I ain't seen him in years."

"Okay," Ellie said. "It's okay with me. Oh keeee doah keeee." She pushed her hair back and looked out the window. "I'm gonna get a new bathing suit for the beach."

We got a room that night in a motel outside of Beaumont. Ellie watched some MTV where all these kids wore suits that were too big and had ratty, don't-give-a-damn haircuts. They were pissed off about something, like maybe they'd been given the haircuts while they were passed out or something. Well, they don't make those shows for the likes of me, and I was feeling restless. I thought of sliding out and getting a couple of quick beers in the motel's bar, but I didn't want to leave Ellie, and I sure wasn't taking her into a bar where a lot of horny salesmen and truckers were sitting around getting drunk and looking for trouble.

"Ellie," I said, "Let's turn the TV off and get some sleep now. I want to get up early tomorrow and get moving."

"Okay, Lou," Ellie said, immediately turning the TV off. She's a good girl, Ellie. I walked over, kissed her cheek, and said, "You might want to brush your teeth, honey."

She got up and went into the bathroom. I went on over to my own bed, slid out of my jeans, and quick slipped under the sheets.

I closed my eyes, pretending sleep, and I heard Ellie cut the light switch and crawl into her own bed. She likes to sleep in the raw—it's how she was raised—and I do what I can to keep my thoughts away from that arena. There's no sex between Ellie and me, you understand. My job is watching over her, and that requires all my concentration. It's a dark, hungry world, in case you ain't noticed.

MALCOLM

I believe that modern psychological thought doesn't give boredom the motivational weight it deserves. I think that the answer to a lot of human behavior is, quite simply, boredom. Boredom drives people to bad marriages, and theft, and treachery and violence. I see it every day.

I think boredom explains my own actions following my visit with Hank Greer.

Almost as soon as I left the Greer farm, the sky darkened, and the first raindrops burst against the car windshield like overripe grapes. It rained solidly for five days, often violently. On Saturday, I decided to go to the Unitarian Church's potluck singles supper, but the rain was still a grim onslaught that obscured the parking lot, and I discovered that I had no heart for the occasion. I sat in the church lot, turned the windshield wipers off, and watched the street lamps melt under dark sheets of water.

I drove home without entering the church, telling myself that at least I had avoided Miss Mitford's discussion of her son's orthodontic work and Miss Adrian Blakely's vacuous New Age nonsense. Upon returning to my home, I went directly to my bedroom, donned my pajamas and crawled under the covers.

My mother knocked on the door and popped her head in. "You are home early," she said.

I asked her if there was anything wrong with that. She conceded that there wasn't, with an air of great reproach, and then retreated, leaving me to guilt and a sudden suffocating dissatisfaction with my life. I tried to read a novel I had recently purchased in which the President of the United States is revealed to be a serial killer and cross-dresser, but my mind kept drifting to Eleanor Greer.

Where had she gone?

Boredom, you see. I was massively sick of my narrow bed, my dismal circle of acquaintances, my tedious job, the incessant rain. And so I got up, went to the closet, and found—as I thought I might—the telephone number of Hank Greer. It was in the pocket of my suit coat, written on a Post-It note.

I called him. He didn't seem surprised to hear from me, despite the hour (it was after ten in the evening). I was not surprised by his reaction either, since I've come to understand that most people will answer any question that someone in an official capacity asks them. People like to believe that those in charge have good reasons for what they do.

I asked Hank about Eleanor Greer's companion. What was his name again? Lou Willis. And how, exactly, had Hank come to know this Willis?

He knew him from high school.

The next day, I drove out to their farm where Hank's pretty wife handed me the yearbook and said, "Hank says for you to be careful with this." I drove off with Hank Greer's 1966 Davis High School yearbook and parked a mile down the road. Turning the pages to the senior class pictures, I found Lou Willis' picture, looking like Paul McCartney must have looked at around the same time, a chubby-cheeked teenager of the goggle-eyed, sincere school of lying ("It wasn't me!" his picture seemed to say). Underneath the picture, an unsung laureate of yearbook character analysis had written the three allotted adjectives: *thoughtful—loyal—polite.*

I studied the thoughtful, loyal, polite Willis and thought of Eleanor Greer and the charred mattress in her brother's backyard. Lou Willis' expression of wronged innocence haunted me.

On Wednesday, during lunch, I made some calls. Mrs. Hamilton, who is every bit as sharp as she is exasperating, watched me hang up the phone, and then said, "You are hot on the trail, aren't you? You are like that private eye on television, only you just make phone calls while he has to drive all over town. Of course, I guess it wouldn't make much of a show, if he was on the phone all the time."

I smiled at Mrs. Hamilton. "The phone is mightier than the Ford," I said, delighting myself with the brilliance of my wit. In my three days back at work, I had amused myself by trying to unravel the mystery of Eleanor Greer's whereabouts. I justified the time spent on this matter as being job-related, although, of course, this wasn't precisely true. If Eleanor Greer had chosen to leave the County, that was her business, not the County's.

I realized that Eleanor herself wasn't going to be any help. She had no relatives, other than her brother, and he didn't know where she was. I'd have to find Lou Willis, and Eleanor would be with him.

I spent my spare moments navigating Briscoe County's various agencies in the frail vessel of my telephone. I was overturned a number of times—numbers that did not work, clerks who seemed incapable of understanding English, and secretaries who were as tight-fisted with information as the CIA—but I was able to prevail upon a number of people to fax me documents, and I learned that Lou Willis had run afoul of the law as a teenager (public drunkenness, petty theft), had enlisted and gone to Vietnam but been discharged five months later for medical reasons, had received vocational training and obtained work at Sloan's Air Conditioning where, according to County records, he was still employed. He was married.

I called Sloan's and was told that Lou Willis did not work there. Three weeks ago, he had failed to come in on Monday, never called, and his phone was disconnected.

I asked the man on the phone if he had any idea where Lou Willis might have gone. He didn't, but added, "He wasn't worth a shit after his wife left him. He was a good worker before that—didn't have much of a personality, but he was a good worker."

I called the wife ("Ex," she said, "It's a done thing. We filed and the clock's running."). The ex-Mrs. Willis was living in Waco. She hadn't seen Lou Willis either, but she gave me the name of the nursing home where Mrs. Eunice Willis, Lou's mother, resided. "He was close to his mother," she said. "He was always closest to her. When she had her stroke, that's when he changed, got real distant. He blamed himself, and he blamed me too. Said I should have let her come live with us."

When I called the nursing home, the ward clerk said, "Honey, she can't talk on phones. You want to see her, you come on out." On Saturday, I did just that. The day was warm and bright, and I rolled the window down and let all the promise of spring into the car, but the nursing home took the heart out of me. The building was low to the ground, and the walls were painted a pale green. I felt as though I were underwater, a queasy sensation. A nurse led me to Mrs. Willis's room. I passed a large, dimly lit area where a dozen elderly people, their bodies formless under blankets and robes, were watching a talk show on a giant TV screen. Mrs. Eunice Willis, a small, gnarled woman lost in a landscape of pillows, thought I was her son. I was unable to disabuse her of this notion, and when I finally attempted to leave, realizing that no information was forthcoming from this source, she refused to let me go, clutching my arm with surprising strength.

"What do you say?" she shouted. "What do you say, Lou Willis?"

I looked at the nurse for aid, but the nurse scowled and nodded. "Go on," the nurse said.

"What?" I asked, trying to back away from the elderly Mrs. Willis without dragging her onto the floor.

The nurse rolled her eyes. "Just tell her you love her, for goodness sakes," the nurse whispered.

"I love you, Mom," I said, and made my escape.

This robbed me of some enthusiasm for the investigation, but I managed to stop at the nurse's station and ask if there were any relatives other than Lou Willis.

There was, it turned out, a husband. But he wasn't in the neighborhood. He lived in Florida. There was a telephone number.

I called the number for Roy Willis on Monday. I said I was calling regarding his son.

I was told that Lou Willis was not there. "He's out right now," I was told. "He's gone to the beach with his girlfriend. He ain't in any kind of trouble, is he? I told him he couldn't stay here if he was in trouble. I'm too old for trouble."

I put the phone down and said, out loud, "He's gone to the beach with his girlfriend."

"What are you talking about?" Mrs. Hamilton asked.

"I'm Sherlock Holmes," I told her.

LOU

Ellie had her heart set on this pink bikini bathing suit that a good-sized cockroach would have had a hard time hiding under. "Sorry," I said. "I'm afraid not." I laid down the law, and she finally settled for a more modest one-piece. She sulked some.

"You are an old fart," she said. "You don't know anything about fashion."

"What we are talking about here has always been in fashion," I said. "And I know all about it, honey. Believe me."

I bought myself some swim trunks. They were camouflage, which was kind of a joke. "I reckon I'll be able to sneak up on any ocean-going VC." I laughed. Ellie laughed too, not for the joke but because she found my white body, with its monkey-brown arms, a hoot.

We stopped at a drugstore and loaded up on beach stuff: a float, suntan lotion, sunglasses, towels, even a portable radio so we could listen to music.

I hadn't been to the ocean since I was a kid when St. John's Summer Camp had packed a bunch of us on a bus and taken us to Galveston. I felt like a kid again, and I worked the radio until I got one of those oldies stations, and lay back and let the sun blaze away, squinting through my shades at a big vacation sun.

I'd been worried about seeing Dad; didn't know what kind of reception I'd get—although he's the one that run off, so, logically, I'm the one with a right to a grudge. It was all right, though.

Dad's like me, he don't go in for big displays of emotion, hugging and that sort of stuff. But he shook my hand and hugged Ellie, and his eyes got bright, and he kept saying, "Well, there's been some water over the goddam dam, hasn't there?" and rocking back in his chair and shooting me one beer after another and generally making me welcome.

The old man was looking pretty good for his age. His hair was blacker than I remembered, and I guess he dyed it cause his eyebrows were as gray as frost, but he still had all his teeth and his shoulders were still broad.

The house wasn't bad either, a two-story wood frame with a big attic fan that made a terrible clatter when you first turned it on but then settled down. It was the sort of house a real estate salesman would call a "fixer-upper" and Dad was putting new cabinets in the kitchen, and the floor on the screened-in porch was tore up.

"I'm busy as a hooker at a convention of Bible salesmen," Dad said, and he grinned his old Irish grin, and winked at Ellie. "If you'll excuse that comparison, Miss Greer."

Ellie giggled.

After I got her settled in the guest room and kissed her goodnight, I went back downstairs and told Dad I was sleeping on the sofa.

He raised his eyebrows. I could see he was after more information, but I didn't feel obliged to supply it.

"I'll just sleep here," I said. "If it's all right."

"Well sure," he said, and he went off and came back with some sheets. "You ain't in any trouble with the law?" he asked, and I thought then we might have an argument, but I just said, "No, the law don't have any interest in me," and he nodded and went off.

The next morning, I woke and smelled coffee perking, and just lay there, enjoying that hopeful smell. Hearing voices overhead, I sat up and hauled my pants on and went upstairs.

Dad was standing at the door to Ellie's room. He was telling the story about the time our dog Samson was whupped by an opossum. It's a good story and he tells it good, and I could hear Ellie laughing. I walked quick past him, said, "Excuse us," and shut the door. Ellie had pulled the sheet up around her, but, laughing and all, she'd let it slip—and like I say, she sleeps in the raw.

"Better get dressed," I said.

The beach calmed me down. There's something about the way the ocean just goes on and on that is reassuring.

"Look at those little birds there," I said to Ellie. "Don't they look like windup toys? You figure if they fell over, their legs would keep on kicking."

"I need for you to put this suntan lotion on my back, Lou Willis," Ellie said, rolling over on her stomach. With her rhinestone sunglasses, she looked like a movie star.

I rubbed the lotion in while Ellie continued to talk. She talked about how we should go to Disney World since we were in Florida. She had picked up a brochure somewhere. "I want to meet Mickey Mouse," she said. I didn't say anything, and I guess Ellie took that as me saying no, because she started to pout. "There ain't nothing wrong with meeting Mickey. There ain't no harm in Mickey. Mickey Mouse is a gentleman, Lou Willis, and you can't say different, and you know it."

Ellie has a style of argument that doesn't require my comments. I let her go on, and when she finally stopped, I said, "I guess we could drive to Disney World. Why not?"

That cheered her up right away, and she turned around and gave me a hug and a kiss. She smelled like sunlight and towels fresh out of a dryer, and I almost lost my balance and fell into her, but somehow I got to my feet.

"I'm going for a swim, honey," I said, and I turned and ran straight into the ocean, and threw myself into the hard, cold waves, and swam straight out past the breakers, and floated on my back and closed my eyes and listened to the seagulls holler and waited for a feeling of doom to leave me. And I thought it had, but just when I thought that, I was suddenly sure that a shark the size of an eighteen-wheeler was right under me. I swam back to shore, heart beating like crazy. Every inch of the way, I felt it follow me, down there in the blackness, a big, angry, upside-down God eyeing a sinner.

Nothing happened though. I still had my legs, and it felt good, putting each foot down on the scalding sand. But the blanket was empty; Ellie was gone.

I knew I was right about the feeling then. I was wrong about the shark, but I was right about the danger. I grabbed up a towel, wrapped the clasp knife in it and jogged toward the boardwalk.

I didn't have to think twice which way Ellie would go. It would be the crowds and the glitter that would draw her. The other direction was older folks, parents with children and old women looking for seashells. I wouldn't find Ellie there.

The beaches were crowded. I walked past a big, pink hotel where teenagers were playing frisbee and a volleyball game was going full tilt, with lots of blonde girls screaming and laughing, like a soda pop commercial. It seemed to me that a lot of those girls were technically naked.

I was feeling dizzy and wasn't seeing right. Too much sunlight was falling, like grain spilling out of a silo. I thought I'd have to sit down and clear my head, but just then I saw her. She was standing at a hot dog stand, eating a hot dog and talking to a big, tanned fellow wearing those Speedo swim trunks that are a joke on modesty.

"Ellie," I shouted.

She turned and waved, all innocent and glad to see me.

She stood up a little on the balls of her feet when she waved, jumped a little, and I knew she was truly glad to see me and that she didn't know how scared I was for her.

"Lou," she said, when I came up to her, "these are the best hot dogs."

I looked past her at the blond boy who was wearing the dollar-an-inch bathing suit. He had what I call a squirrel-in-the-middle of the road smile, meaning it could go any way, that smile. I gave him a cold look.

"Lou, this here is Howie," Ellie said. "He was telling me how he plays in a rock band."

"I guess that would impress some folks," I said.

Howie's smile went away. "I wasn't trying to impress anyone," he said. I could see then that he was one of those fellows who liked a fight.

"It's good you wasn't," I said. Howie frowned.

"Oh Lou," Ellie said. "I wish I was in a rock band. You know I can sing." She finished her hot dog, crumpled the wax paper, and tossed it in a wire trash bin. Then, suddenly, she turned. "Last one in is a rotten egg!" she shouted, and she bolted for the ocean.

I clutched Howie's arm. "Settle for being a rotten egg," I said. "Take my advice."

He glared at me now. His eyelashes were too long for a real fighter. I felt tired.

"Take your hand off me," he said.

I took my hand off fast. "I didn't mean anything," I said, thinking I could still stop things somehow.

"I'm going for a swim," he said.

Fear came on me again. I was desperate. "Don't go!" A fat lady, walking by, gave me a quick, startled look and then moved on. I wasn't thinking, and I grabbed his arm again. I was talking fast. "Look, I was just out there. There's a big old shark out there. I swear. I'm gonna fetch Ellie right now. It's too dangerous."

It was a feeble attempt, I admit. He yanked his arm away, and poked a finger at my chest. "You old fucking hayseed," he said. "I told you I was going for a swim. Now get out of my way before I kick your ass."

I got out of his way, watched him jog down to the surf, jog out to the first wave and dive into it. You could tell he'd done it a few times. He looked comfortable in the ocean.

I traipsed on down to the tide, keeping my head down. A lot of black, tangled seaweed lay at my feet, like something a cat would cough up. *People shouldn't go swimming in this stuff,* I thought. I kept studying the seaweed, unwilling to look up, but finally I had to. Sure enough, he was out there with Ellie, the two of them bobbing up and down, not more than two feet from each other.

I threw the towel away, let the sea grab it. Holding the clasp knife close, I marched into the dirty water. I didn't look up, didn't give them another look. I knew exactly where they were. I swam past a couple of young boys who were horsing around. I swam with long, slow strokes.

I can hold my breath for a long time. Ma says I was a hollering baby, so maybe that's how I come by my good lungs. Anyway, I slid under the water, and started out. I swam blind, with my eyes closed tight, and when I finally stuck my head up, I was no more than five feet from the back of handsome Howie's head. If Ellie had been looking at him, she would have seen me, but she was swimming back toward the shore, and I thought: *Now or never.*

I filled my lungs and sunk back under. I flipped my knife out and frog-kicked forward.

I caught him around the waist, and he was hairless and sort of slick with suntan oil, and he leaped half out of the

111

water, but I was expecting that, and he spun right into the knife and it opened him up. I thought I could hear the blood hissing out of him, like steam. My hands felt scalded by it. I went down with him, and we rolled like circus acrobats under a bigtop full of black water. I could feel him shrinking in my arms, and I thought: *If I just wait a bit I can put him in my pocket.* But I was out of air, and I had to let him go and fight for the surface. I guess, if Ellie had been there, she would have seen in my eyes what I'd done. But I was a lot farther out from shore, and I couldn't make her out. When I did find her, she was helping a little girl build a sand castle.

"Where did your friend Howie go?" I asked.

Ellie shrugged her shoulders. "We got to make a moat for this castle, Lou," she said.

"Maybe a shark got him" I said. "I saw a big one out there."

That night, me and Dad and Ellie were eating supper, TV dinners the old man cooked in the microwave, making a big production of it, like he was some fancy chef. He had Ellie giggling every time he called her mademoiselle.

"You young folks should go out to a nightclub, go dancing," he said. "That's what I'd do." He elbowed me and gave me that slow wink that I remembered growing up. I never did care for it. "If I had a pretty girl I'd take her dancing every night."

"Lou don't dance," Ellie said.

Dad's eyebrows went up. "He don't. It's hard to credit he's my son. Maybe his momma was seeing a preacher behind my back. I'm a dancing fool myself." He spun around, one hand on his hip. "I would dance them women dizzy."

Dad went out into the living room, and when he came back, this old, corny rockabilly music followed him.

He reached over and tugged Ellie out of her chair. Still laughing, they danced around the kitchen. My old man wiggled his butt and shouted at me: "It's a crime not letting this girl dance."

I went to the fridge and got a beer. I opened it and poured its contents down my throat. I sat back down. *Let them have their fun*, I thought, and I did. I let them go through about four numbers while I drank another beer. Then I thought: *That's enough.* I went into the living room and shut off the record player.

"Hey!" Dad shouted, coming into the room. Beads of sweat dotted his temples and his shirt stuck to him. "You are forgetting whose house this is."

"Well," I said, "I appreciate your hospitality. I just don't want you to overdo it." I walked up to him and looked him in the eyes. "The hospitality," I said. "I don't want you to overdo the hospitality."

He glared back at me, like he might want to make something of it, but he decided against it, shrugged his shoulders, and went back into the kitchen. I heard him say to Ellie, "That boy has always had a briar up his butt." I heard Ellie laugh.

MALCOLM

Ten miles south of Gainesville, I pulled the car to the side of the road, got out and vomited.

I am not a good traveler. I do not like driving for hours on end, stopping only to relieve oneself in restrooms defaced with various homosexual come-ons, and living marginally on expensive synthetic road food. I do not like having my life imperiled by amphetamine-deranged truck drivers or having to seek out some interstate gas station every hour in order to scrub the slime of a thousand smashed insects— whose guts could, no doubt, serve as the ultimate super glue—from my windshield.

These bugs were an industry. They were called love bugs because they mated on the highway, huge clouds of them. I bought this small blue and white can of stuff designed especially to dissolve their innards. The service stations also sold screens to put over your car's grill so that the bugs wouldn't fly into your radiator and cause your car to overheat and blow up. Never underestimate nature. I bought one of the screens, too.

Having vomited, I leaned against my car and stared out at what appeared to be water buffalo and large, white birds. Dots swam before my eyes, dots which proved to be small, malevolent mosquitoes. I slapped at them and climbed back into the car.

This was all my mother's fault. I had mentioned to her that I might drive to Florida, and she had responded with unwarranted negativity.

"You don't want to go to Florida," she said. When I was away at college, my mother had gone to Miami with my father, their first vacation in years. This was a year before their divorce. Relations were already strained.

"Florida is hell," my mother said. In Florida, according to my mother, the air conditioning does not work, the showers have no hot water, hotel room service is nonexistent, the beaches are crowded and dangerous, the heat is unbearable. An odor of dead fish hangs over the state like an Old Testament curse.

I told her I did not plan on going to Miami, that my intention was to drive down the gulf coast to St. Petersburg.

"Texas has a gulf coast," my mother argued. "It's closer and cleaner and cheaper."

The argument managed to escalate until I found myself saying, "I don't want to discuss it. I'm going."

And so I discovered that what had been idle, out-loud daydreaming became, thanks to my mother's adamant opposition, action.

Sick and disgusted with myself, I wasn't about to turn back. Besides, I was almost there. A few more hours and I'd be in St. Petersburg.

What then? Well, I'd had time to think about that on the way down. Granted, discovering the whereabouts of Eleanor Greer and Lou Willis had been a sort of exercise, a test of my investigative powers. Granted, also, that I was making this trip in childish defiance of my mother's wishes. Still. . . . Perhaps there was a purpose. I am not a very religious man—I am, after all, a Unitarian, and even there my attendance is erratic—but perhaps I was meant to make this trip. Eleanor Greer was an innocent; nature had not granted her those powers of discernment which other young women could rely on to keep them out of the clutches of unsavory males. There was no telling what sort of jeopardy she was in. And, being powerless and alone in this world, she would have no way of extricating herself from the situation. I could offer her help, prompted only by compassion and genuine concern for her welfare. I could approach her and say, "Eleanor, it's me, Malcolm Blair. Are you all right? Do you want to go home?" And, if she did, I would take her back to her brother. There was a very real possibility that she would want that, that my appearance would, in fact, be her salvation.

Stopping at a gas station, I got a Coke to wash the acrid taste from my mouth. I was beginning to feel better. I was, after all, a man with a mission. Hardships were to be endured in the pursuit of a good cause. I purchased another bottle of love bug solvent and pushed on.

LOU

You can't let down your guard in this world. Not for a minute. I came out of the drugstore—I guess I was in there five minutes—and Ellie was on the sidewalk hugging this fellow.

She saw me coming, and I guess she read the look in my eyes, because she put her hands on her hips and frowned. She was wearing a bright yellow sun dress and a Panama hat, and if she'd gone to heaven that minute Jesus himself would have caught his breath.

"Now Lou," she said, "This is Dr. Blair, and you can just stop thinking what you are thinking, because he is my case worker at Taylor, and I won't have your ugly thoughts."

I didn't say anything, and this Blair fellow, who was a skinny guy with a brown mustache, was mumbling how he wasn't actually a doctor, was actually only a bachelor, and how he was there on vacation and wasn't it a coincidence, you know, running into Miss Greer? I had rarely seen a person lie so badly. It made me uncomfortable, and I almost shouted, "Don't!" He was wearing a suit. The temperature had to be in the eighties, but he had this brown, crumpled suit, and he was even wearing a tie, so that looking at him was painful.

"This is Lou," Ellie said, and he reached out his hand to shake mine. I took it.

"Pleased to meet you," I said, shaking his hand, which was a little like holding a dead frog.

He was going on about what a big coincidence it was, running into Ellie, how he was just looking out the window at the shops and there she was. I hummed a tune in my head to keep from listening closely and maybe saying something before I could put the brakes on it.

116

I shot Ellie a dirty look when she said we could all do something together, like go to the beach or out to dinner. She gave him Dad's telephone number too, which he wrote down in a little black address book.

I was steamed, and when we got back in the car, I roared out of the parking lot, ran a red light, and gave this old geezer, who was crossing the street real slow, a reason to put some spark back in his step.

"Lou Willis, there ain't nothing to be mad about," Ellie said.

I didn't listen, just hunched over that wheel and mashed the accelerator.

"You stop that!" Ellie shouted. "You just stop!"

I had the window rolled down, and hot wind, like a tarp flapping in a hurricane, crowded out her voice. *I'll drive as fast as I please*, I thought.

I forgot—I guess because it had not happened for some time—that Ellie has a mind of her own.

Suddenly she screamed—my heart just stopped in the middle of a beat—and she flung her door open. I guess I was going eighty-five; I was up there somewhere where the car starts to shake, flying down this two-lane highway through weedy, scrub-pine country, cloudless and full of heat. Ellie screamed and I thought: *Oh God!*

I hit the brake, and we fishtailed down the highway, and the tires squealed, and the steering wheel jerked in my hands. We turned sideways to the highway, and I saw a lot of cattle standing around a pond, still as a painting, and we seemed to lift up a little in the air, and I thought: *We are gonna roll.*

The car kept going around, though. If there had been another car on that highway, we would have had to hit it. But there wasn't, and I kept my foot slammed on the brake and we bounced up across a ditch and came to rest against a fence.

I cut the engine and turned to Ellie. I started in, "You almost—"

But Ellie wasn't there. Her door was wide open, and I could see a patch of black water, a busted-up shrub, and some weeds.

I couldn't get the door open on my side, so I crawled out the passenger side.

My throat was too dry to shout her name, and anyway, I guess I was afraid silence would come back at me. I couldn't stand that.

I scrambled back out to the road and looked down it. There wasn't anything but flat highway and blue sky with one high, circling buzzard.

I killed her, I thought. I fell right to my knees, like God himself had blindsided me.

"Lou," Ellie shouted. I turned quick, and there she was, coming out of the field behind the car.

I ran to her and hugged her. Her cheek was bleeding. "I can't find my hat," she said.

"Are you okay?" I asked. My voice rattled like loose change.

Ellie Greer giggled, reached out and pushed my hair back off my forehead. "Did I scare you?"

"Well, I guess you did," I said, feeling anger come over me. "I guess—"

Ellie didn't wait for my lecture. She put her face up to mine, not more than three inches so I could see the truth in her eyes, and she said, "You just hush, Lou Willis. I just want you to remember this: I want you to remember that I am not riding in any old runaway speeding car."

I shut up. I'd forgot what Ellie was capable of.

The engine started right up, and we got back on the high-way. We didn't say anything for awhile.

Finally, Ellie said, "I can't make you like Dr. Blair, but you don't have to be rude to him."

"Well, it just seems fishy to me," I said. "Him showing up out of nowhere. Maybe he's trying to cut you out of some welfare."

"You are so suspicious," Ellie said. "Dr. Blair wouldn't do anything like that. He is a gentleman."

I was getting a little sick of that "gentleman" stuff. That Blair, with his sweaty suit and his slickster's mustache, looked like the kind of a guy who would sell you a car with a busted block—and you'd deserve it if you was fool enough to believe him.

"How do you explain him turning up?" I asked Ellie. "The world ain't *that* small, you know."

Ellie considered this, frowning and studying the highway. "Maybe he's going to Disney World," she said, "same as us."

"Disney World is way off in Orlando. How come he's here?"

She folded her arms. "You said we could go to Disney World. Don't tell me different now, Lou Willis. Don't go telling me it is 'way off'."

I can't argue with Ellie. There's no sense trying. I can never get a handle on her rules.

For the next week, Ellie and me didn't do anything but go to the beach and eat and watch videos on Dad's VCR. You'd think a schedule like that would relax a fellow, but my stomach felt like it was full of rusty nails, and when the screen door would slam, my heart would jump under my tongue.

I guess the truth is, I am not a man much suited for doing nothing. Working for Sloan's wasn't heaven, but it kept me occupied, and there was real satisfaction in fixing a thing. Old Henke, my boss, was a bastard who would have stole the pencils from a blind man's cup, but I was mostly out on calls, so I didn't have to see him, and if he was shaving my hours some, it wasn't worth an ulcer. We'd get into it once a month maybe, some kind of argument, and I'd stay away from the place for a day or two. But then I'd get restless and come back—and he'd be glad to have me. He had black hair that he slicked down with grease and parted in the middle, and I'd come back in, and there he'd be, like a dog that's rolled in a grease pit, and he'd show his false teeth and say, "Bygones will be bygones," and he'd slap me on the back, and I'd consider spitting on his shiny wingtips, but I'd just nod my head and say, "Yeah, Henke. Whatever you say."

I guess I'm just a working man, and I'll endure a lot to get on with a job.

So on Sunday, I looked through the want ads, and I circled a few of them.

On Monday, I dressed in a clean work shirt and jeans and told Ellie I'd be back in a couple of hours. She was watching morning cartoons and eating Cheerios so she just looked up quick and said, "Okay." Dad was already out back working in the garden, and I went out to tell him I was going.

"I was wondering when you was gonna think about work," he said. "I knew you wasn't born with a silver spoon in your mouth." He laughed and whacked a garden glove against his overalls, raising a cloud of dust.

I was about sick of Dad's company. Fact is, I was beginning to understand what a good thing his running off years ago had been. Two nights ago, he had taken Ellie to a nightclub. He knew how much I was opposed to that, but he did it, bringing the subject up in a sneaky, joking way. "I am thinking of going dancing," he had said. "Only thing is: I'm afraid some woman might take advantage of me. Sometimes I drink too much, and my judgment fails me. I was hoping you kids could come along and sort of watch out for me."

"Ellie ain't going to any nightclub," I had said, and that's where I made my mistake, of course. Ellie heard that, and it stiffened her backbone.

"I'll do what I please," she said.

It was downhill from there, and I lost that fight. I let them go and sat home watching a video. I couldn't tell you what it was. They came back late, in a cloud of beer fumes, and Dad had his arm around Ellie's waist, and neither of them was too steady.

I decided then that I'd had my limit. It was time to get a place of my own.

Pulling out of the driveway, I saw a car parked across the street, one of those silver, Jap cars. Someone was sitting in the driver's seat. It didn't mean anything until I got back that afternoon—feeling pretty good because it looked like Eskimo Air Conditioning was gonna hire me—and that same Jap car was there and the same dude in sunglasses was behind the wheel.

Of course, it took about ten seconds, now that the car had my attention, to notice the Texas plates.

He ain't real clever, is he? I thought.

MALCOLM

I am, I suppose, a stubborn person. I know my mother would not hesitate to say I am the world's most stubborn person. It is true that when I encounter an obstacle, my resolve is strengthened rather than weakened.

Arriving in St. Petersburg and checking into a motel, I

immediately caught a cold. I think it was the air conditioning in combination with the brutal road trip that weakened my resistance and left me prey to the innumerable viruses that must, of course, lurk in motels and public restrooms.

The morning after my arrival, I could barely crawl out of bed, and then only to vomit and retire again. Later in the day, I managed to make it to the lobby where I was able to purchase a number of cold remedies and retreat again to my room.

For three days I felt rotten: feverish, disoriented. As is often the case when I'm ill, I had dreadful doubts regarding the course of my life. This most recent adventure seemed particularly foolhardy and was perhaps a manifestation of some real mental and emotional breakdown.

On the fourth day I was able to order something more substantial than soup, and on the fifth day I was able to go out into the sunlight and purchase a map of St. Petersburg. That afternoon I drove down the shaded street where Eleanor and Lou were staying with Lou's father. The house number was prominently displayed on the mailbox, which was a white and grey two-story in need of a paint job. The neighborhood was, however, respectable, and I had mixed feelings about that. I suppose I had been hoping to rescue Eleanor from a ghetto.

Finding the house was enough for that day. I was still weakened by my bout of illness, and I drove back to my motel and went to bed early, setting the alarm for seven.

In the morning, I drove back to the house, parking several blocks up on the other side of the street. I had no experience in shadowing people, but luck was on my side. Eleanor, wearing a yellow dress that would have allowed one to find her in a crowded stadium, came out of the house almost immediately—as though she had been waiting for my arrival. She was followed by a broad-chested man in a white t-shirt and brown and green mottled swim trunks. I was too far away to make out his features, but I assumed, from the proprietary way in which he ushered Eleanor into the big maroon car, that this was Lou Willis.

That morning they went to the beach. For the next three days, I was unable to approach Eleanor. They were either at the beach, in a restaurant, or in some store. Willis rarely left her side, and when he did, he was never gone long.

Your true investigator, your professional, no doubt has more patience than I do. It was a mistake, I know, to approach Eleanor when I did, and I'm sure a certain furtive quality was apparent when I whispered to her: "Miss Greer!"

She gave a little squeak of surprise, and then turned. "Golly, it's Dr. Blair!" I am not, of course, a doctor, but it is a title Eleanor persists in using, I suppose because she is used to people in authority who do, in fact, possess such titles.

Before I could say a word, before I could ask if she required my help—and ask it in a tactful and generous fashion that would put her completely at ease and so obtain her utter confidence—Lou Willis came out of the store.

Eleanor, a girl of natural exuberance, was hugging me when he came out, and the general coolness of his demeanor suggested how unhappy he was with this show of innocent affection.

No, I had no time to ask Eleanor anything regarding her circumstances. But I am a professional. Noticing the nuances of personal interaction is my job. How often have I seen couples in my office who were at cross-purposes? A thousand times. Ten thousand times. The tension between Eleanor Greer and Lou Willis was palpable. If he were not actually holding her against her will, he was certainly exerting psychological pressures which young Eleanor, a child emotionally and mentally, would have no resources for combating. I was sure, instantly, that I had done the right thing in coming.

And I didn't like Lou Willis's looks, quite frankly. His appearance hadn't improved since that high school photo. The years had hollowed his cheeks and pushed his eyes back under a knobby ridge of bone. His eyes still had that surprised look, that feigned innocence, but now they held a kind of crazy, unblinking outrage that said: *I'm not about to let you get away with whatever you are getting away with.*

I didn't like the way he moved, either, always shifting his weight from one foot to the other with a nervous, brawler's air, leaning forward a little, a sly, am-I-crowding-you smile and his chin angled up. He had rope-like, hard muscles that gave no sense of physical well-being but simply seemed like flesh pushed to the limits, and although I was several inches taller, I knew I was no match for the man in any sort of physical encounter.

I don't think he believed that I just happened to be in St. Petersburg and just happened to run into Eleanor. The story did lack credibility, and in my defense I can only say that I had never intended to tell it, hoped never to meet Lou Willis.

Obviously, I would have to be more circumspect in the future. I returned to shadowing Eleanor and Lou, waiting for that moment when I could have more time to gracefully interrogate Eleanor to say, "Eleanor, do you want me to take you back home?"

I thought I was exerting great caution in this matter, but when my car door was yanked open and I tumbled onto the street, only to be yanked erect by Lou Willis—who smelled of some pungent cologne—I realized that I had been taking a number of things for granted.

"Hey hoss," Willis said, "This is sure a coincidence, ain't it."

Willis pushed me back against the hood of my car and released me. My sunglasses had fallen off. I watched Willis crush them under his boot and then pick them up.

"Here you go," he said.

I took them and slipped them in the pocket of my shirt.

"Go on and put them back on," he said. "It's still right sunny."

I put the glasses back on. The plastic lenses were still in place, but now I was looking through a spider web, sun flaring in the cracks. This broken vision brought it all home. I was in big trouble.

"Look," I said, "I just need to talk to Miss Greer about vocational training. It's unclear, for instance, if she intends to establish new residency or—"

Willis laughed. "Mr. Case Worker, you came all the way to Florida on my tax money? I'm delighted to see a dollar goes so far. Makes me feel good about giving it."

"Well—" I said. I was beginning to realize the advantage of fabricating lies in advance. I was at a loss for words. Lou Willis, however, would probably not have been interested in anything I had to say.

"Just get in the car," he said. "We are going for a drive."

"No," I said, "really. No."

He pulled a gun out then; I don't know where it came from, unless he'd had it stuck in his belt. Casually, rubbing my neck a little with his other hand, he put that gun against my forehead and said, "I won't say it again. I will just shoot you dead and walk away and drive out of here before you have slid all the way to the ground, and that will be it. I don't care much, and if you got any ear for the truth, you'll know you are hearing it now."

I believed him. I got in the car.

LOU

We drove out of town. Whenever we came to a road that looked sorrier than the one we were on, I had him turn. Pretty soon we were on this tan stretch of nothing. The only gas station we passed was boarded up and one of the pumps lay flat on its back, its hose and nozzle next to it like a dead snake. We passed two children and a dog that was bigger than both of them. And then we just drove along, with nothing but scrub pine and some of those scruffy cabbage palms for company.

"Mr. Case Worker," I said, "what brings you all the way to Florida? I'd like a straight answer if you please."

He was leaning over the wheel like there was a pain in his stomach, and he said, quiet so I could hardly hear him: "I can't see to drive with these sunglasses on."

"Well, take them off then. Goddam, don't you have any sense? You want to get us both killed?" I laughed.

He took the glasses off and turned and looked at me. "I came to see Miss Greer because I feared she was in trouble. My fears were obviously justified."

I shook my head. This fellow really was crazy. "Goddam if you ain't something," I said. "You feared she was in trouble! Did you now!" He didn't say anything, just stiffened a little and looked back at the road. "What were you gonna do about her trouble? Were you gonna give her some food stamps?" I shook my head.

"What do you know about her anyway?" I asked.

"I suspect I know more about her than you do," he said. He had a kind of haughty tone, there, which I had to admire. I mean, the gun was resting in my lap. He was wearing the same old suit, but he didn't have a tie on—he was starting to let himself go, I guess.

"I bet Juvenile told you all about her. I know what they

say. I've heard all them words you folks have to describe anyone a little different. You can call a person any name you want and not know anything." I was working myself up. I guess I had to, really. "No sir, you don't know shit about Ellie Greer! You ask her brother—you ask Hank Greer—to show you that big old burn scar on his back. Hank Greer got that from his daddy when that sonofabitch laid a red-hot skillet on him. And what Hank got ain't the half of what Ellie got."

"I am aware of Eleanor's unfortunate childhood," he said, starch in his voice. Oh, for a skinny, prissy sort of a fellow he had some backbone.

"Turn here," I said, pointing to a dirt road up to the left. He turned, and we rocked along in a cloud of dust.

I kept an eye out, and when we came to a place where we could pull off the road, I had him pull off and stop. "You can leave the keys in the car," I said. "We won't be but a minute."

"What are you going to do?" he asked. I marched him through a field of tall grass that was patrolled by big, low-flying dragonflies. Up ahead I saw a clump of pines and a little cow pond.

"I don't know what I'm gonna do," I said. "It's not like I have a lot of choices." If Ma had heard me, she would have said I was feeling sorry for myself. "You got a bladder full of the poor-me's," she would have said.

We walked down to the cow pond. Up close, it smelled bad.

"You ever been fishing?" I asked him.

"Oh course," he said. "I did quite a bit of fishing as a boy."

"Well now," I said. "You reckon there are fish in this pond?"

"Yes, I would think so. The dragonflies are a good sign,"

he said. "They would indicate an abundant mosquito population, something for the small fry to feed on."

Well, I thought, *this fellow thinks we are on a field trip.*

"That's very interesting," I said. "I wonder if you would mind stepping into the water, then. You know, taking a closer look. I might go fishing here sometime, and I wouldn't want it to be a lot of wasted energy."

He just blinked at me.

"You might take your jacket off," I said. "You wouldn't want it to get wet."

"No," he said.

I moved a little closer to him and said, "All right. Suit yourself." I pointed the gun straight at his head.

"Let me get my jacket off," he said.

I nodded, and watched him take his jacket off. He had an awkward time of it, like the jacket was too small.

He handed me the jacket, his arm coming up, straight out, and there was something else besides that brown suit jacket in his hand. A cloud of wet ammonia-stinking spray hit me in the face, and my eyes caught on fire. I staggered backwards, and that first shock of fire exploded into something that made a kind of napalm *whump* in my brain.

I fell back on the ground, screaming like a stuck pig, rolling around in the mud and the weeds. It had to be luck, cause I didn't have two wits to rub together, but I got on my feet again and ran into the water, and plunged right under, like a nest of hornets was after me.

Well, these hornets could swim.

I believe some of my memories were burnt up forever. I don't have them any more. They are gone, and they might have been important memories, info I could use in a jam, but I'll never know what's gone and what's still here. Pain ate them right up.

I kept ducking my head under water, trying to cool my eyes, and I stayed there for some time. I didn't give any thought to Mr. Case Worker until the pain had let up a bit. Then I looked around, but he was gone. I crawled back up on the bank and squinted at the world. I wasn't blind after all. I could see, although the world hurt to look at. The fellow's jacket was still on the ground, and so was my gun, and so was this blue and white can with the words LOVE BUG LIQUIDIZER on the side. I flung that can out into the water and lay back on the ground, letting the sun dry me off.

It was curious, but I didn't feel any particular urgency to get up and run after or away from something. I guess I felt that whatever was going to come was coming, and there wasn't anything I could do about it.

I would have laid there even longer, but some ants wanted me off their property and they lit into the back of my neck. I sat up quick, smacked them, and decided it was time to move. For some reason—I don't know why—I put that fellow's suit jacket on and then put the gun in the pocket and walked back out to the road. The Jap car was gone, naturally, and I walked on down the dirt road.

I figured I'd be walking all the way back to town, but a trucker picked me up.

"You look kind of poorly," he said.

I didn't say anything, but he was one of these fellows who has got to talk or he'll bust.

"You look like you got the grandaddy of hangovers," he said. "I don't believe I seen eyes that red on a human being."

"Well I hope I made your day," I said.

I still had to walk a mile from where the trucker let me off, and I was beat when I hit the door. Dad and Ellie were sitting watching television, and as I walked by, Dad shouted:

129

"Eskimo Air Conditioning called. I think they want you to go to work for them."

"I'll call them tomorrow," I said, and I walked on upstairs, took a shower, and fell in bed. I slept right through till the next morning. When I woke, Ellie was there beside me, jay naked and on her back, her mouth open.

I gave her a long look, ran my eyes down the whole reckless length of her. Light shot through the blinds, golden ribbons, like an angel God had unwrapped.

I pulled the sheet up around her. She closed her mouth and rolled on her side, winding the sheets round her.

"I don't know," I said. "I don't have a clue." I got out of bed and went into the bathroom. My eyes still didn't look too good.

In the kitchen, Dad had something to say about my looks too, but I didn't have time for it.

I called Eskimo Air and got the boss and he said he could use a fellow like me, but times were tight, and he wasn't sure he could pay me what I was worth. I kept saying, "Uh huh," and when he finally made me an offer, I said I wished I could take it but I had obligations that wouldn't allow me to go so low, and he hummed a bit and made me another offer and I said, "Okay."

He asked if I could start right away, and I said, "Sure."

So I had a job. It was a load of work. I even had to fix the funky van they gave me for service calls. This place was tight with a buck, and some of the tools they gave me were a joke. I bought some tools on my own, took money out of my own pocket. There is nothing worse than trying to work with cheap or broken tools. I will gladly spend my own money to avoid that aggravation.

And the work was good for me. I could have been staying home, waiting for the ax to fall. I kept expecting Mr. Case

Worker to come banging on the door with a dozen cops at his back.

"This fellow tried to kill me," he'd say. He couldn't lay anything on me that would stick, but I didn't fancy the attention of a lot of cops.

I put the gun in a coffee tin and buried it in the backyard, but nobody came around. I finally went back and dug the gun up. I didn't want some kids finding it and maybe hurting themselves.

I stopped worrying about the case worker, decided he had got the message. I liked to think he drove straight back to Texas, saying, all the while: "I got to be helping folks in Texas. That's my true calling. Folks in Florida are out of my jurisdiction, and I'm glad Mr. Willis pointed it out."

Of course, I wasn't going to let the matter of my eyes just pass. The fellow had definitely done something to them. The redness went away by mid-week, but I couldn't see things properly anymore. Things were sharp enough, but sometimes there would be holes in what I was seeing, little whirlwinds of churning, electric air. I didn't care for that effect. You bet I had something to settle with that boy. But I learned a long time ago that letting a little time pass is the best way to handle it. I might drive through Texas in a year or two, and that's when I'd look him up. He might be walking out of his office or even mowing his lawn on a Saturday, and I'd come right up to him and say, "You don't remember me?" And probably he wouldn't, at first, but I'd watch the recollection come into his eyes. I'd enjoy that.

With work, with any new job, you have to get into a rhythm. There's an adjustment period, while your body gets used to the pace. I was wore out that first week, not so much with the work itself but with the way they had you keep track of your hours and call in all the time. It was a nuisance.

I'd come home in the evenings, drink a couple of beers, and collapse.

Dad started taking Ellie to clubs. I wasn't crazy about that, and sometimes they wouldn't get home until I was already asleep.

"Girl's got to have some fun," Dad said. "She's got to get out a little bit."

On the weekend, I just wanted to lay back, but Ellie insisted we go somewhere.

"What do you have in mind?" I asked.

What she had in mind was that goddam Disney World. I explained to her that it wasn't a weekend trip, that it would take longer than that. "It's all the way on the other side of the state," I said. We had a good fight then.

Dad surprised me. He agreed. "It's a long way, Ellie, and that Mickey Mouse will turn your pockets inside out quicker than a Times Square whore."

Well, Ellie wouldn't hear anything mean about that mouse, so she screamed and ran up the stairs to her room, the door slamming shut.

I was worried that Ellie might do something rash, but Dad patted my shoulder and said, "I got a plan."

"What's that?" I said.

But Dad always loved a secret, and he gave me another one of those broad winks and didn't elaborate. He went upstairs and I heard him knock on Ellie's door.

An hour or so later, he came back down, and Ellie was with him. She wasn't quite ready to give up sulking, but he had calmed her down. And half an hour later, he had her laughing with his imitation of Oprah.

On Sunday, I took Ellie to a movie. I asked Dad if he'd like to come along, but he said, "No, you kids need some time to yourselves." We went and saw this movie about a woman detective with a funny name. It was about how everyone thought her name was funny and made jokes about it. I fell asleep, but Ellie said the movie was good and told me the story on the way home, and it certainly sounded interesting.

Then, on Monday at dinner, Dad sprung his surprise on me. I could see he had already talked it over with Ellie. He had got tickets for Barney Baker's Fabulous Funland up in Bayport. The plan was to drive up to Bayport on Wednesday and stay until Saturday.

Dad explained it. "It ain't as crowded during the week. And I got a friend runs a motel up there. He'll give us a cut rate."

Ellie piped in, like she'd been coached, I reckon. "They got animals and rides and those cartoon characters from the Barney Baker show and a house full of mirrors and Monster Mountain and . . ."

"I guess you ain't noticed that I work," I said.

Ellie shot right in, breathless, "You could tell them it's an emergency."

It wasn't Ellie's fault, and I knew it. I glared at my old man. "You folks have a good time. You take a lot of pictures so it'll be just like I was there too."

I tried not to think about it. There wasn't anything I could do about it. On Tuesday after work, I went and talked to this fellow who had a garage apartment for rent. It was reasonable, and I told him I'd be back on Friday with a deposit. I would have my own surprise for Dad. "Ellie and me are moving out," I'd say. "Surprise."

Tuesday night, watching Ellie rush around packing her things, I got to feeling peculiar, like she was leaving forever, and she must have noticed, because she came over and sat in my lap and hugged me. "You just tell me not to go, and I won't," she said.

Well, I'm no fool, so of course I said I hoped she had a good time. But I got up real early Wednesday morning and drove off in the van before Dad or Ellie stirred. I just didn't fancy all the excitement.

Around noon, I was drinking a glass of ice tea with an old woman who said she was originally from Albany, New York and might go back there any second. "I might go down to the bus station this very night and leave," she told me. "The phone might be ringing, and I might walk right by it and go down to the bus station."

"You should," I said.

"What's that?"

I didn't repeat it. I didn't care what she did, really. I'd been working at a fast pace all morning, racing from one service call to the next, and suddenly, sitting down, I couldn't tell you why I was bothering.

"Well, I better be going," I said. "I'm driving up to Bayport to that amusement park."

"Barney Baker's. My husband and I went there once. It was great fun."

MALCOLM

I suppose I should have gone to the police. But I am familiar with a certain official mindset, and any interview with the police would, I feared, be an interrogation. "What brings you to Florida?" they would ask.

I would be hard pressed to give them a satisfactory explanation. In these cynical times, concern for a fellow human being lacks the self-interest required to make it a plausible motive for doing anything.

I did not want to be misinterpreted.

Besides, although I was convinced that Lou Willis had intended to kill me, I knew that my certainty wasn't enough to get any real action. All the police might do is scare Willis off, and he would take Eleanor with him.

As I lay there in my hotel room, recovering from my ordeal—and thanking God and man for the invention of love bugs and love bug solvent—I realized that I was Eleanor's only hope. Lou Willis had demonstrated that he was a killer, and I was the only one who could separate Ellie from him. Who else knew? Who else cared?

I am not a courageous man. As I lay there in bed, I shook. I am not a drinker, but I called room service and availed myself of several stiff gin and tonics.

I grabbed the remote from the end table and turned the television on. I pushed the mute button and watched the images. Silent television has a calming affect. A foppish boy-man smirked at me from behind a desk. "David," I said to the silent late night host, "You can believe it or not, but I am going to rescue Eleanor Greer." No doubt the alcohol contributed to the effect; I felt a rush of righteous invulnerability.

In the morning, I felt somewhat less invulnerable, but my resolve was unshaken.

This time I would move with more caution. I would not take Lou Willis for granted. He possessed a low cunning and intelligence that I had underestimated. I wouldn't underestimate him again.

I rented a car. If I were going to follow him, I obviously couldn't do it in the Honda. He would recognize it. I felt a sharp pang of embarrassment when I thought of how glibly

I had parked across the street from his house—with Texas plates! Did I think Lou Willis was blind?

A look at my street map showed that there was only one route Willis could take from his father's house to the main street, and so, hunkered down in a large, nondescript rental car—the sort of faded luxury car that St. Pete's large population of oldsters drove—I was able to pick Willis up as he left the house without watching the house itself. Indeed, I was parked a good quarter of a mile from it, in the parking lot of a supermarket, and could see Willis coming, the old, maroon Impala seeming to exude evil as it came out of the shady, oak-lined street and into the bustling sunlight.

I wasn't going to jump the gun this time. I wasn't going to try to contact Eleanor until I knew I could do it without fear of interruption.

Then Lou Willis got a job, and it looked like I'd be able to make my move. He was away all day—going to work in a company van with the words "Eskimo Air" on the side and a cartoon of an Eskimo outside an igloo. The van was a less ominous vehicle than the Impala, but knowing Willis was inside that van colored the Eskimo's smile, made it seem cruel and calculating.

I waited a week. Not once did Willis come home during the day. I called my office on Friday and said I was going to have to stay out another week.

Mrs. Hamilton got on the phone—my supervisor was out—and said, "You only go around once, Malcolm. Don't worry about hurrying back. You're only young once!"

Mrs. Hamilton confided that she had had a few drinks at lunch that day and was thinking of leaving the office early herself. "I'd like to see them try to fire me for leaving early!" she bellowed. I told her I would see her Monday a week and hung up, feeling a little unsettled. Perhaps my presence had

exerted some calming effect on Mrs. Hamilton, had com-
pelled her to practice some restraint. No telling what shape
things would be in by the time I got back. Well, it couldn't
be helped.

The next week, I resumed my vigil. Monday and Tuesday,
Willis left for work at seven and returned home at six-thirty.
On Wednesday, I had just pulled into the parking lot with a
cup of coffee when I spied the van coming down the street.
It was just six in the morning. I watched the van rattle by and
waited another two hours and drove to Roy Willis' house.

I parked across the street, took some deep breaths, and
prepared to get out of the car. My heart was pounding. I had
thought the scene through several times, but it never had
sufficient clarity in my imagination.

Eleanor trusted me, and that, I hoped, would be all I
needed. "You've got to come with me immediately," I
would say. Nothing more.

But what about Roy Willis? He might want something
more in the way of an explanation. I had seen him several
times during my first ill-fated surveillance, and he looked
like a tough customer. Lou Willis was, after all, the man's
son.

I decided I would just have to hope for the best, and I
started to open the car door.

The door of the Willis house opened, and Roy Willis
stepped out, Eleanor following on his heels. They were both
carrying suitcases. I watched them toss the luggage into the
trunk of the Impala, watched Roy Willis flick a cigarette into
the driveway, and watched them get into the car and pull
out of the driveway.

I followed, of course.

What was going on here? Were they running away?

Roy Willis drove recklessly, changing lanes frequently,

and it was all I could do to keep up with him. They got on 19 and headed north.

They stayed on 19 for an hour or so and then swooped into the right lane and shot down the exit ramp. The sign read: BAYPORT. The Impala slowed abruptly, and I was right up behind them and worried that Eleanor might turn and see me. I got in the left lane and passed, keeping an eye on them in the rearview mirror. We went along for fifteen minutes or so, down a highway flanked with billboards and souvenir shops, and suddenly the car turned left into a pink-stucco motel. I pulled into a gas station and looked back.

The motel had a big faded sign cut in the shape of a seagull. GULL'S REST MOTEL, it read. I filled the tank of my car, got some pretzels to munch on, and drove back to take a look.

I saw the Impala immediately, and before I could consider my next move, a door opened and Eleanor and Roy Willis came out and jumped back into the car. Eleanor had changed into shorts and a green, sleeveless blouse, and Roy Willis had donned a Hawaiian shirt that didn't suit him, that made him look like some Mafia kingpin hiding out in Acapulco.

An hour later, I was eating cotton candy while three large skunks wearing sombreros played guitars and sang a song whose message was that all men—and skunks, I suppose—were brothers. This was the entertainment while waiting for the next haunted train ride up Monster Mountain. I could see Eleanor up ahead in the crowd, and I didn't think that my sunglasses were sufficient disguise should she look my way. The cotton candy offered some cover, although I have always been partial to cotton candy and so was rapidly destroying this source of concealment.

I was in Barney Baker's Fabulous Funland, an amusement park on the outskirts of Bayport. The place was what Disney

World might have been if it had been conceived by con men and ex-carnival hucksters. You couldn't make a move without someone selling you a ticket to something. You had to have a ticket to walk down Jungle Alley, and you had to purchase a ticket to take the ferry across Piranha River—and it seemed to me that you had to go across that river if you wanted to get *anywhere.*

I confess, I enjoyed Ferret Warren, where we all crawled through tunnels that undulated and changed directions while we were in them, but the Breath-Robbing Body Bouncer was not my cup of tea, and I despised the Dogs On Ice show. And I lost five dollars trying to get a mechanical snake to devour my stuffed mouse.

And, of course, none of this was getting me any closer to achieving my goal. Roy Willis stuck close to Eleanor, and I saw no way I could approach her. The funhouse atmosphere overexcited me, and I feared I might do something reckless, so I decided to leave. I needed to find a motel and register, and now seemed as good a time as any to do that. Obviously Eleanor and Roy Willis intended to stay overnight or they would not have checked into a motel themselves. My time would be better spent resting and devising a plan for tomorrow.

Still, I felt frustrated. I needed, somehow, to seize this opportunity, to take advantage of Eleanor's separation from Lou Willis.

On the way out of the park, a large hamster asked if I had a cigarette, and I had to tell him I didn't smoke. I know he was a hamster, because I asked. There was a querulous note in his response: "Hamlet Hamster," he said. "I'm Hamlet Hamster, for Christ's sakes! You been living on the moon, or what?"

I had paid money to enter this park, and I didn't need to

be abused by its employees. "If you are so famous, you can afford your own cigarettes," I said. "Besides, studies have shown that smoking is hazardous to hamsters."

"You are a riot," he said. "You should get a job as a clown." His voice seemed younger now that I'd stirred him up. I imagined a tall, surly teenager under that costume.

I spoke with dignity. "I am quite happy with my present profession, thank you." I walked away, before he could answer.

"I am a social worker," I said to myself as I drove back to the motel. "I am a man of action."

And, as though saying the words unlocked the door, a plan presented itself. That boy had given me an idea. I saw a clear path to Eleanor's rescue.

Tomorrow, Eleanor Greer and I would be on our way to Texas.

LOU

I found the Gull's Rest Motel easy enough. It wasn't any great shakes of a place. Dad had made it sound like his friend worked at the Ritz, but this was the sort of place that looked better if it was two in the morning and you'd been driving twelve hours.

The man at the check-in desk didn't want to tell me anything. He looked like the kind of person my old man would have for a friend; he had a kind of jailhouse squint and kept leaning back like he had to keep as much distance between us as he could in case I tried to pull a fast one.

I convinced him that I was who I said I was, but I had to show him my driver's license to do it—"You don't favor your dad," he kept saying—and then I had to listen to some stories about stuff he and the old man had done a million years ago.

"That's interesting," I finally said, "but I'm wore out. If you will give me a key, I will go on in the room and wait for them to come back."

Well, he didn't know if he could do that, because he wasn't the owner of this establishment, and the room had been rented to two people, not three, and he might get in trouble.

I knew what he was getting at, and I didn't want to run all around the track with him, so I just handed him a twenty and he fetched the key.

The room had two big old beds, and it was better than I would have expected, except for the wallpaper which was different kinds of fishes, realistic, like photographs. I didn't go for the way they seemed to circle, made me feel like bait, and I would have preferred flowers or a stripe pattern.

I went and took a shower, and that perked me up. I didn't fancy just waiting around for them to show, so I went out and found a bar.

I got pinned down in there. I don't know just how it happened, but I couldn't get out. It was cool and damp, with most of the light coming from an old jukebox that had lots of real country singers, folks like George Jones and Hank Williams and people who had really suffered—people who knew a thing or two about pain, and I'm not talking a trip to the dentist.

I tried to leave once (I remember) but the sunlight was like a fire that blew me back inside. I didn't try it again until it was dark, and then I guess I wanted to be sure it was going to stay dark, so I had a few more beers, and then I forgot what was the emergency and why I had to leave right away, and then they closed the place up and I found the van and drove back to the motel.

I slipped the key in the lock, quiet so as not to wake anyone up, but, as it turned out, there wasn't anyone sleeping.

I didn't like what I saw, and for awhile I guess, I lost control.

I sat on the edge of the bed for what must have been an hour. I stared at Dad's feet, which were bare and stuck out from under the sheet, but I don't know that I thought about him, or much of anything else. I just let my brain idle in neutral.

I was aware that Ellie was talking, but I couldn't seem to focus on her words.

Finally I heard her say, "Your daddy ain't no gentleman, Lou."

"Honey," I said, "He ain't nothing. He's dead."

We were both quiet, studying the old man's feet as though they might offer up an opinion on the situation.

I felt bad about it. But Dad should have known better than to try anything with my Ellie. I guess he figured I wasn't around so he was safe. I cursed myself for not seeing it coming. I'd felt it all along. What was that shark if it wasn't old Dad?

"I killed old Dad," I said. "I come all the way to Florida to visit him, and I killed him."

Ellie hugged me then, and I was aware that she was naked under the bathrobe. "Get dressed, honey," I said. "We can't just sit here all night."

Ellie and me drove to an all night supermarket, and I got some packing tape and some of those big green trash bags—and some room freshener too. I don't like to speak ill of the dead, but Dad had left a powerful bad smell behind when he departed this world. We sprayed clouds of pine scent into the air. Then I pulled one of the big plastic bags over Dad's feet and jerked another down over his head and taped them together. I went outside and opened the Impala's trunk.

"You are going to have to help me tote him," I said.

"Okay," Ellie said. Ellie isn't a girl to shirk a duty.

Together we hauled him into the trunk, and I slammed the trunk shut.

"I'm exhausted," I said. I didn't feel drunk anymore, not one bit, but I had that hollow weariness that seems like there's not enough sleep in the world to feed it.

"I'm sorry," Ellie said.

"It ain't your fault, Ellie."

I lay back on the pillow and I was out. I dreamed I was on a mountain, in a forest—I guess that was the pine scent working on my subconscious—and I come across this little fox in a trap. Only the fox was Ellie, and I knew that, the way you know things in a dream, and I went to get the trap off, but she bit my hand. "Ellie," I said, "You got to stop that or I'll never get this off."

And then I heard something coming through the trees. It was big, whatever was coming, and I could hear the brush crackle around it, and a wind came up and shook the trees around us and I woke screaming: "It's too much!"

"Lou Willis," Ellie said, coming over to my bed and laying a hand on my forehead, "You have the night sweats."

"I do." I was shivering.

"You shouldn't drink so much," she said, and I agreed.

It might sound cold to some, but we went to the amusement park the next day. I wasn't gonna have another chance at it, not soon, and it sure didn't make any difference to Dad. Besides, if we'd just bolted, Dad's motel friend might wonder.

I got a kick out of the way Ellie took to being a tour guide.

She had been the day before, so she was a big authority on everything.

"These hot dogs are too spicy," she would say. "Don't bother with them." Or: "Don't go buying any souvenirs in Cannibal Canyon; you can buy the same stuff for half price from the drugstore near our motel."

I had a good time. I'm not really one for rides and games and all that carnival stuff, but watching Ellie laugh, watching the way her hair would fly on the roller coaster ride or the way her mouth would open in wonder when Mr. Whistlebee popped the colored balloons and white birds flew out, all that made my heart light as a dandelion seed.

I let my guard down. The laughter fooled me. It distracted me.

I had to take a leak. I couldn't have been gone more than three minutes. That's how things always happen: in the blink of an eye. You hitch your fly back up, turn around, and tragedy has struck. The Bible don't have nothing to tell me on that count.

I came back out. I had left Ellie in Cowboy Courtyard where a fellow in fancy cowboy getup was doing rope tricks. He had a little tiny dog with him that would jump around and bark. It was the kind of dog that a real cowboy would be ashamed to own, but I didn't say that to Ellie. I was glad she was happy and enjoying herself.

I panicked when I couldn't find her right off. I calmed myself down and thought: She's just gone off to the restroom herself. I made myself wait. But she didn't come back.

I started to run, first one way, then another. There were too many people everywhere, and I knocked some of them over without intending to. That got the attention of a skinny security guard, who chased after me, shouting. I didn't have time for him, though, and I raced up the steps of this big fairy castle, taking those steps two, three at a time, and I made it to the top where a lot of people were getting a bird's-eye view of the park, and I pushed past them and leaned out over the knobby, broken-tooth stonework and tried to pick Ellie out. And maybe I've got radar for her, because I found her almost immediately. She was in the parking lot. She was getting into a big old blue car, maybe an old Lincoln or another one of those luxury gas-guzzlers. One of the park's costumed animals was holding the door for her.

Just then the security guard laid a hand on my shoulder.

"What's your problem, buddy?" he asked.

"That's my girlfriend," I said, pointing at the parking lot. He squinted, following my finger. "There. She's getting into that blue car. A rat or something is holding the door open."

"That's no rat," he said. "That's Hamlet Hamster." He sounded surprised himself.

I pushed him away and ran back down the stairs. I can move fast when I've a mind to, and I got to the parking lot before they'd made it to the main gate. I jumped in my van and went after them. I gained some time by flying past the parking attendant without paying. He shouted after me.

I saw the car up ahead in traffic—it *was* a Lincoln—and slowed a little. I wouldn't lose them now. I took some deep breaths. Okay, okay. *Let's just ease back,* I thought, *and see what the story is here.*

MALCOLM

It was a brilliant plan, and it worked. I got up early the next morning—I had rented a room at the nearby Holiday Inn—and drove quickly to the park. As soon as it opened, I sought out Hamlet Hamster.

Hamlet Hamster proved to be a skinny teenager, one who had shaved his head to nubbly baldness and wore a small, gold earring. "I don't know," he said. "I could get in a lot of trouble."

What he meant, of course, was that I would have to meet his exorbitant fee if I wanted to rent the costume. I didn't even bargain, just forked over seventy-five dollars. He looked a little unhappy. The alacrity with which I produced the money made him think, no doubt, that I would have been good for even more. He was, I could see, the sort of person who always feels ill-used.

He led me to a locker room where he removed the costume. He wore nothing but his underwear, and he advised me to do the same. "It's hot inside this muther," he said.

I thanked him for this advice but didn't take it. I didn't intend to be in the costume long, only long enough to spirit Eleanor away.

Eleanor showed up at ten. By then I understood the teenager's advice. I felt as though I were being boiled in a burlap bag. My vision was severely limited, and I was required to pat children on the head, be photographed with obese, lewd women, and wave at crowds. I realized that the last occupant may have shaved his head for comfort rather than adolescent style. My hair felt like a thicket of dirty briars, and rivulets of sweat ran down the back of my neck.

I forgot all about this when she arrived. Eleanor alone might have made me forget my discomfort, but she was accompanied by Lou Willis! Willis' father was nowhere in evidence—but that was a small thing. Lou Willis!

The man terrified me. He seemed to look right at me and I thought: *He sees me!* and it was all I could do to keep from turning and running.

But, of course, he didn't see me. He saw Hamlet Hamster.

I was invisible. The plan remained a good one; I had only to carry it out. And I had, after all, already made a seventy-five dollar investment toward the success of my mission. No turning back.

My chance came when Lou Willis went off to the restroom. I followed him, and when I saw him go in the men's room, I raced back to Eleanor.

I tapped her on the shoulder, trying my best not to scare her while still wishing to convey the urgency of the situation.

"Eleanor," I whispered. "Eleanor."

"Hamlet Hamster!" she shouted. She hugged me.

I whispered into her ear: "Eleanor, you've got to come with me. I don't have time to explain, just follow me, okay?"

Eleanor said, "Okay."

Eleanor kept up with me. Running was strenuous in the costume, and I thought the heat would finish me, but I ran through the main gate and out into the parking lot. Eleanor was giggling.

"There!" I shouted, pointing to my rental car. "Quickly."

Eleanor ducked under my arm and slid into the passenger's seat without hesitating.

I ran around to the driver's side and got in.

I was terrified that Lou Willis was right behind us, and I had a bad moment when I realized that my car keys were in my pocket. I pulled off the hairy mittens that were Hamlet Hamster's paws. The rest of my costume—not counting the head—was a one-piece, like those pajamas with feet that little kids wear, and I was going to have to get back out of the car and get this costume off—and Lou Willis would saunter up and shoot me.

"Eleanor," I said. "Do you have a nail clipper?"

She stared at me, her mouth open and shook her head no.

I am in trouble here, I thought.

"I just use this to trim em," Ellie said, producing the pocket knife.

I grabbed the knife and sawed through the threads at a seam, jammed my hand through the opening and retrieved my keys.

I heard Eleanor say, "Gosh."

I pulled out and drove up to the parking attendant. I started to fumble in my pocket for the parking fee, but the attendant waved me through, and I realized that I was a celebrity.

The man hollered after me: "Jimmy! You better be careful. You're gonna have a wreck if you try to drive with that mask on."

I saw, immediately, what he meant. I was driving while looking through a keyhole, no peripheral vision. I had to turn my whole upper body, making sure my shoulders moved on an even plane, or I lost one or another of the eye holes. At the first red light, I wrenched the head off and tossed it into the back seat.

Eleanor gasped. "Dr. Blair!"

I looked at her. "It's okay, Eleanor. I had to resort to this disguise to get you away from Lou Willis. I have every reason to believe that man is dangerous."

Eleanor's eyes were wide. She shook her head, raised a hand to her forehead. "Who would have believed it?" she said. "Dr. Blair is Hamlet Hamster! If I told my friends, if I told them this story . . . they'd say, they'd say: 'Ellie you are taking bad drugs!' That's what they'd say."

"Your brother's worried about you," I said.

"He is? Hank?"

"Yes, I thought I'd better take you back to Texas. I can't make you go, of course, but I have every reason to believe that Lou Willis is a very dangerous man."

"Well, he is," Eleanor said. "That's true. He'll say it himself."

We drove on. Getting out of the parking lot had disoriented me, and I wasn't sure how to get to 19.

I heard Eleanor say, "I can't believe it," again.

Then I saw The Gull's Rest Motel up ahead and Eleanor said: "I can't go to Texas without my things! You got to stop!"

I was reluctant to do that, but Eleanor was insistent.

I turned into the motel. "You'll have to be quick."

"Sure," Eleanor said.

I waited in the car with the engine on. The place seemed pretty much deserted. There was a cart with towels and sheets parked right next to Eleanor's room so maid service must have been around. I decided to shed my costume before anyone showed up, and I got out of the car and wriggled out of my hamster skin. I had the costume crumpled down around my ankles, and I was leaning against the side of the car when the Eskimo Air van pulled in.

My throat closed to a pinhole. "Eleanor!" I shouted, but it was hardly a noise at all.

I yanked the costume off my feet and kicked it away. I jumped back in the car and threw it in reverse.

I crashed into the front of the van, and the collision banged me against the dash. I suppose I hadn't closed the door properly, because it flew open, and I bounced out onto the pavement.

Lou Willis was already out of his van, and I could see the gun in his hand.

He walked over to me and looked down. "We met before," he said.

I heard an odd, rattling noise and looked up to see the maid's cart full of towels rolling slowly toward us.

The cart caught Lou's attention too. He looked away for a second and shouted, "Ellie!"

I looked too. Eleanor must have bumped the cart, sending

149

it on its jittery course as she struggled out the door. She was dragging a mattress through the door. She turned, saw us, and said, "Give me a hand with this mattress."

"Ellie," Lou said, running up to her, "get back inside now, you hear?"

I scrambled back in the car. It had stalled out when I hit the van, but the engine caught when I turned the key. Lou Willis heard, and turned back to me. He raised the gun. The cart was right in front of him, and he started to push it away.

I couldn't back up; the van blocked me.

I think I screamed. I know I made some kind of noise and then threw the car in drive and stomped the accelerator.

The car leaped forward, slammed into the cart and kept going. Towels and sheets flew into the air, flapping like monstrous gulls. The Lincoln stalled again, and I climbed out. Lou Willis was slumped over the grill in a welter of white towels.

Eleanor looked up at me. There were tears in her eyes. "Help me with this mattress, Dr. Blair."

"Eleanor, we have to leave." I took her by her shoulder. "Do you have the keys to that car?" I asked, pointing at the Impala. I knew the Lincoln wouldn't be going anywhere.

"Roy always keeps his keys under the seat."

This proved to be the case.

I found them and started the car. "Please," I said. "Hurry."

Eleanor frowned, looked at the mattress, and then turned away, ran to the car, and jumped in.

"It doesn't matter, I guess," she said.

I looked in the rearview mirror as we pulled out into traffic. Someone had run out of the office and was running toward the Lincoln and Lou Willis. I thought I saw Lou Willis move.

150

LOU

They wrapped about ten pounds of tape around my ribs, and I was moving around like I was eighty years old. I guess it didn't matter; I wasn't going anywhere where speed was required.

If it had just been me, the car, and the wall, I wouldn't be going anywhere at all. That case worker wasn't playing games.

"The cleaning lady's cart absorbed most of the impact," one of the cops told me. "You were lucky," he said.

"I feel lucky," I said.

They thought I might have a concussion too. I had cracked the back of my head against the wall. But X-rays didn't show anything, and so the doctor handed me over to the cops, and they took me downtown.

It was uncomfortable, sitting around with my chest tied so tight that each breath was an effort.

They asked me a lot of questions. Finally, one of them said: "You know anyone named Walter Reed?"

"No," I said.

"He worked in a gas station," the cop said. "Some sorry son of a bitch shot him in cold blood for a couple of dollars."

I didn't say anything. Then he shifted subjects, wanted to know if I knew about a truck driver killed at a rest stop outside of Temple.

He asked if I wanted a lawyer, and I said I didn't. He started talking about fingerprints, witnesses. "We can place you at both scenes," the cop said.

"Where's the girl?" one of them asked.

"What girl?"

"Your accomplice," the cop said.

I shook my head. My heart felt like someone was holding

it in his fist. I couldn't let them get the wrong idea. "It wasn't like that," I said.

"How was it?" he asked. So I told him. I knew I wasn't telling them anything they didn't know. They had me tell it a couple of times, and then the next day another fellow came around, this one in a suit, and he had me tell it all again.

I finished my piece and he said: "You shot the truck driver with this gun."

He held the gun up, and I said, "Sure."

"He was coming toward you, and you shot him."

"That's what I said."

"Was Miss Greer with you when this happened?"

"Naw, she didn't see it. She had run off."

"There's no possibility that it was Miss Greer who shot this truck driver, then?"

I laughed. "Ellie wouldn't hurt a fly." This was true; Ellie didn't hold with harming flies or any kind of bug or animal.

The detective stood up. "You might be interested to know that Mr. Sterling"—that was the truck driver's name—"was shot at close range. The barrel of the pistol was probably touching his throat when the trigger was pulled." He turned and walked to the door. He paused. "And it wasn't this gun. It was a smaller calibre." He looked at me, said, "I just thought you might be interested," and left.

They came and took me back to my cell. That detective was wrong, though. I wasn't interested.

I had other things on my mind. I knew I wasn't going anywhere for a long time, and I was worried sick about Ellie. That case worker proved to have some backbone, but I still didn't think he was capable of really looking out for Ellie. She was just a child out there, and she needed a load of protection.

Who was gonna do it now?

MALCOLM

I drove north up 19 with my heart pounding. I had run a man down, and now I was fleeing the scene. I kept thinking: *I'll stop and phone the police. I'll tell them I panicked. I'm sure it happens all the time.*

But I didn't do that. Instead I drove on up to Gainesville, got on the interstate, and kept heading north.

Eleanor reached over and turned the radio on. She found a country station and turned it up loud.

I was in shock, I suppose. The day was oppressively bright, cheerful.

Eleanor said, "I could use something to eat."

We stopped at a restaurant where the food took a backseat to postcards and paperweights made out seashells.

I wasn't hungry anyway, and I ate my watery hot dog without enthusiasm. Eleanor, however, devoured a hamburger, french fries, and a chocolate milk shake and said, "I could use a piece of pie."

I don't believe she was fully aware of our plight. The terrible events at the motel had left her seemingly unaffected. Of course, her behavior might be a defense mechanism. She might actually be in shock. I am no psychologist, and I'm not capable of evaluating such things. She did not seem traumatized. Although I was unable to follow her words closely, she seemed to be chatting easily about the various rides and wonders found at Barney Baker's Funland.

I swallowed the last, leaden bite of my hot dog and said, "Eleanor, I believe we will have to call the police."

"Lou doesn't like police," she said. I sympathized, for a moment, with Lou Willis. "Police are always telling you what to do. Lou don't like that."

I wasn't looking forward to it myself. "I'm afraid we have

to talk to them." I didn't go to a telephone though. Instead, I paid the check, and we got back into the car, and we got back on I-75.

I was still trying to sort things out when the wail of the siren made me look up. The flashing lights in my rearview mirror told me the decision was out of my hands. The police had arrived. I was relieved.

"Do you know how fast you were going?" the officer asked.

I had been stopped for speeding.

"No officer," I said, "but—"

My right ear exploded, my cheek was instantly scalded, and the policeman was gone from my window.

Eleanor Greer had leaned across my shoulder and shot him with a small, silver pistol which she was now demurely returning to her purse.

I pushed the door open and fell out onto the side of the road. The cop lay on his back. There was blood all over his face. His sunglasses were still on. Behind me, a big semi-truck was pulling off the road.

"Hurry!" Eleanor screamed.

I jumped back in the car and drove away.

"Take the exit," Eleanor shouted.

I took country roads, turning whenever a new one presented itself.

Finally I pulled the car to the side of the road and threw up in a ditch. Eleanor climbed out of the car too and stood beside me. "It's that hot dog," she said. "I don't ever eat hot dogs when I'm gonna be going on a trip. Car riding and hot dogs don't mix."

"Eleanor," I said. "Why did you shoot that police officer?"

She smiled. "Well, I could see you weren't going to. He had the drop on you."

Well, I thought, *well, well, well, well, well.* That explained everything. I felt abandoned, emptied of all faith and conviction. It seemed of no consequence what I did next. My illusions were like so many shards of glass from a picture window some vandal has smashed. I got back in the car, waited for Eleanor to close her door, and drove off down the country road. Perhaps I would seek out the police station in the next town. Perhaps I wouldn't.

Just then the car made a mechanical grunt and the telltale *whunk, whunk, whunk* of a blown tire forced me to let up on the accelerator.

"Flat tire," I said to Eleanor.

"Lou was meaning to buy new tires," she said. That was no consolation.

I got out and opened the trunk.

"That's Roy," Eleanor said.

I peeled back the plastic bag to reveal that, indeed, I was in the presence of the pale, departed Roy Willis. There was a small round hole in his hairy chest.

"I had to shoot him," Eleanor said.

I nodded my head in agreement. I didn't say anything. Perhaps Eleanor sensed a certain skepticism in my agreement.

"I did," she said. "He got fresh. Lou wasn't around, so he thought he could take advantage of me."

"He was wrong," I said.

I rolled the body out of the way and dragged the spare out of its well.

I changed the tire, throwing the old one in with Roy, and banged the trunk down.

We drove on.

"Good as new," Eleanor said.

Finally, we came to a small town, its main street lined

with shady oaks. It was a peaceful town, and I didn't want to burden it with my troubles.

I looked at the map again. Eleanor peered over my shoulder.

"That's Orlando." She touched the map with her finger. "We could keep going on this road and we'd be in Orlando."

"Why would be want to do that?" I asked.

Eleanor laughed. She had a wonderful laugh, so filled with reckless joy. "Silly. You know."

I told her I really didn't know.

"That's where Disney World is!" she shouted. "We could see Mickey Mouse, and Donald, and Cinderella's Castle and Frontier Town." She paused. "Lou said he would take me, but he never did."

Well, I thought, *that's my fault.* "I'm sure he meant to," I said.

Then I thought: *Why not?* Maybe it was just what I needed. Maybe I could talk to Mickey—or Goofy (I think Goofy was always my favorite). I might find Goofy there on Main Street, just standing around, and I could ask him for a minute of his time, and we could sit on the curb, and I could say: "I can't make any sense of it. I'm frankly out of my element. What do you think? Give me your honest opinion. What do you recommend?"

It wasn't much of a plan. I admit that. But it was the best I could do.

"We are going to Disney World," I told Eleanor.

Eleanor squealed with pleasure and I accelerated some, blasting through brittle fields of sunlight, frightening a tattered crow from its roadside kill, and feeling, for the moment, a renewed sense of mission, however spurious, however fleeting.

Snow

Youth is fraught with moral ambiguity. Huge appetites war with high ideals. As one gets older, one's appetites abate somewhat and the moral absolutes get muddied. But there is a tricky period there when young. You wish to think well of yourself while availing yourself of every pleasure in your path.

I was thinking of this yesterday after a student of mine propositioned me. I am a bald, middle-aged man, thirty pounds overweight. I have sinus trouble and tend to walk about with my mouth open so that when I encounter a mirror I am shocked to see an anxious fish of a human gulping for air. I am not—it goes without saying—propositioned often. I teach economics at a small college. I am not a charismatic teacher. Still, sexual attraction is always a curious and surprising phenomenon. This young woman, blonde and pretty, made it clear that she would not be averse to a sexual encounter.

As tactfully as possible, I told her that I was happily married, and that I was flattered but could not accept her kind offer.

In fact—and this is the sad wisdom of middle-age—I knew it would be too much trouble. My life is a series of routines and small expectations that are consistently met. I did not want to jeopardize that.

It wasn't a moral decision at all; it was a decision based on convenience and comfort. Suddenly, these thoughts conjured up the pale, intense face of Alfred Davidson and immediately—the camera of my imagination panning to the right— I saw the smiling, lavishly-freckled face of Sadie Thompson. In my imagination, she was standing slightly behind Davidson and was preparing to shoot him with a rubber band.

I met Davidson and Sadie in the winter of 1967. I had graduated from college that year and obtained work with an accounting firm (Kimberly and Colson) with offices in Washington D.C. In October, we won a government contract, found ourselves severely understaffed, and hired a number of college students—about a dozen I think—to come in in the afternoons.

I was aware of Sadie from the day she started work. She was a plump red-headed girl, with blue eyes and freckles who laughed easily and musically and was inclined to touch you when she talked. An air of suppressed sexual excitement enveloped her, and Fred Ohlson told me, the second week after her arrival, that he was in love with her.

Fred also warned me about Alfred Davidson. "Look out for that guy. He's a pre-mini."

Pre-mini? I was unaware of the term. Fred explained that Davidson—one of our newly hired college students— planned to attend seminary after graduation in the spring; was a pre-ministerial student or, in the shorthand of his more secular colleagues, a pre-mini.

I had not yet met Davidson, so I could not form my own opinion. Fred added, "He's out to get me," which seemed an odd thing to say on several counts. Fred had worked at Kimberly and Colson for two years and was well-liked. Since he was nobody's boss and did his job competently, it was hard to imagine him inspiring this sort of antagonism.

But stranger yet was the notion—implicit in the solemnity with which Fred announced Davidson's intentions—that a part-time employee who had been at the firm for only two weeks could entertain the thought of "getting" Fred, a valued worker.

"Aren't you being a little paranoid?" I said.

"You haven't met Davidson, Alec. Wait till you meet the guy. He's bad news."

I was to meet Davidson a mere three days later when he came to occupy the desk next to mine. I did not know that this was the young man that Fred had warned me about. I observed a skinny, intense fellow with a severe haircut, full, pouty lips, and heavy-lidded eyes that conveyed a truculent air of disdain. He wore a dark suit that was just a bit too small for him, and he did not introduce himself to me, but began stapling bundles of paper together in a frenzy of activity. Thump. Slap. Thump. Slap. Occasionally a staple would misfire, and he would utter one of what I soon discovered was a vast horde of swear-substitutes: "Jeepers!" Thump. "Golly darn!" Thump. Slap. "Jiminy Crickets!" Slap. "Miniver Cheever! Rats! Bog water!"

When he ran out of staples, he spoke to me.

"I'm Alec Macphail," I said, handing him some staples.

He took the staples. "Alfred Davidson," he muttered, head down as he struggled to open the stapler.

"You push here, then pull back," I said, demonstrating. He followed my instructions, the device popped open, and he looked up and thanked me—reluctantly, I think; I got the impression that he was unhappy being the recipient of any assistance, feeling perhaps that it placed him in a position of obligation.

On his break, Davidson wolfed down a baloney sandwich and then gnawed on an apple while studying what was un-

mistakably a Bible. He would draw in on himself while reading it, his thin body stiff with sanctity.

In the days that followed, we rarely spoke to each other but
I came to loathe him despite our limited social commerce.
Listening to his muttered spurious oaths ("Dang nab! Rats!
Phooey! Bobby socks!") I found myself longing to throttle
him. I could not explain this intense dislike to myself, and I
was relieved when events gave me more solid reasons for
despising him.

In the meantime, I found that I too was becoming enam-
ored of Sadie Thompson. She was an incongruous addition
to our office, rather like discovering a songbird in some dank
catacomb—and a fearless songbird at that, for she sang as
though unaware of the grim, matronly women who curdled
at her approach or the disapproving older clerks—the male
equivalent of spinsters—who grimaced every time she said
"fuck." And Sadie said "fuck," or more precisely "fucking,"
a lot. She was serenely unaware of the effect this had on
others, merely using the word to fill out sentences, to give
body to statements that seemed, otherwise, oppressively flat.
Thus she might say, "The fucking snow has fucking ruined
these fucking shoes." She seemed so unmindful of this word
that I liked to imagine her being raised in a household where
soft-voiced solicitous parents urged the tiny child to eat her
fucking peas if she wanted her fucking dessert or to please
turn the fucking TV off as it was time to go to fucking bed.

I was not the only one in love with Sadie. There was Fred,
of course, and several others. Almost arbitrarily—on a good-
humored whim, as it were—Sadie had awarded her favors to
Lonnie Wilson, an unfortunate choice as far as the rest of us
were concerned. Lonnie was a handsome, conceited lout
who fancied himself quite a womanizer and began, immedi-

ately, to tell the rest of us the precise nature of his relationship to Sadie. The relationship was sexual and acrobatic.

We all despised Lonnie's candor in these matters, but it was left to Fred, miserable and half-mad with unrequited love and jealousy, to express his displeasure.

One day our receptionist, Mrs. Alabaster, was shocked when the elevator door opened on our floor to reveal Lonnie and Fred—both wearing the obligatory business suits—rolling on the floor. Fred was on top and hitting Lonnie in the face, but Lonnie, by far the larger of the two, appeared to be slowly strangling Fred with Fred's own tie. According to Mrs. Alabaster, Fred's face was bright red.

Our manager, Mr. Horn, spoke to the combatants, warning them that a reccurrence of such unseemly behavior would lead to their immediate dismissal.

The incident had inspired Davidson to comment.

"What people fail to understand," he said, "is that only the love and fear of God can defeat our animal natures." Davidson nodded his head, as though I had agreed with him. He paused, and his face elongated with moral censure. "You know, Fred Ohlson is an atheist. He is a man actively pursuing Satan's directives. The first day I arrived here, I saw him reading a copy of a magazine devoted to the promotion of a godless society."

"What magazine was that?" I asked, but Davidson didn't answer, being distracted by Sadie, who had come up behind him and was mussing his hair.

"Please cut that out," Davidson said.

For reasons that have always eluded me, some women are drawn to priggish men, and Sadie had started a game of teasing Davidson. Davidson's confusion and frustration were obvious. He blushed.

"Oh Reverend," Sadie giggled in his ear. "You really rev

my engine." She darted away, and Davidson looked around him with the sort of expression I'd seen on dogs caught urinating on the carpet.

It snowed a lot that November, and I seemed to be always digging my car out, scraping ice from the windows, sitting in its frozen interior and listening to the starter cough. The sound always made my chest ache, like listening to an old man with emphysema hack his way through another morning cigarette.

I hated the blackness of mornings, and I felt cold all the time, for the fine dust of frozen snow that lived in the wind would get under my collar and into my shoes. Once chilled, I could not warm myself until I took a hot shower in the evening.

In this dismal state, I found the office insipid. In December, a Christmas tree appeared five feet from my desk, and its artificial cheeriness made suicide seem attractive. I had written my parents telling them I would arrive on the twentieth, but as that day approached and the drive to Pennsylvania through bad weather grew nearer, I contemplated excuses for not going.

Sadie dumped Lonnie, effortlessly and cheerfully, and took up with another office worker, a quiet young man named Webb who was a dark horse in the race for Sadie's affections.

Fred grew yet more despondent, cursing himself for not acting in that instant when Lonnie ceased to have residence in Sadie's heart and Webb had not yet entered.

I tried to console Fred. "It couldn't have been more than a few milliseconds," I said. I had not told him of my own growing infatuation with Sadie. Fred had told me first, and there is an etiquette to these things.

I then witnessed an act of perfidy on the part of Davidson.

At the time I witnessed the act, I did not understand its nature and was at a loss to explain the guilty expression on Davidson's face. All I saw, in fact, was Davidson rooting avidly through Fred's wastebasket, suddenly shouting "Ha!" and retrieving a crumpled piece of paper. Turning to see me studying him, Davidson started, smiled sheepishly, and said, "I almost threw away something I shouldn't have."

I wondered at the time how he had come to discard something in Fred's wastebasket, since's Fred's desk was on the opposite side of the room. But it wasn't one of those things that occupies the mind for long, and I soon forgot it.

One week later, Fred was called into Mr. Horn's office. When he returned from that conference, he was noticeably subdued, and I asked him what had happened. He explained.

He had thrown out one of Mrs. Wardell's letters. Every business that deals with the public has to deal with a certain crazed, demonically-inspired segment. Mrs. Wardell was a wealthy and eccentric client who lived to inflict pain and suffering on the businesses she dealt with. Her letters were not entirely sane creations, but they always required the performance of arduous and ultimately meaningless tasks. Fred Ohlson had been performing these tasks regularly—and now the letters came addressed to him. His duty was clear, and it is no good excuse to say that he was distracted by a broken heart. It is no excuse to say that he was tempted by the knowledge—demonstrated on other occasions—that a failure to respond would end the matter since Mrs. Wardell penned letters in the heat of the moment and then forgot them.

In any event, Fred crumpled this particular letter and tossed it in the wastebasket. Mr. Horn asked if Fred knew of the existence of such a letter, and Fred denied such knowledge. The letter was then produced, and Fred's protestations—shrill with outrage—failed to impress his boss.

"Here is the letter," Mr. Horn said. "It is clear what it requires. Please get on with it."

Fred was convinced that Davidson had seen him toss the letter, had retrieved it, and had brought it to Horn's attention.

I realized that this was, in fact, what I had seen, but I still hesitated to confirm Fred's suspicions. I wrestled with this reticence for a week, and then the whole matter proved irrelevant.

Every business initiates certain rules which seem arbitrary and senseless. Kimberly and Colson demanded that employees stay in the building during breaks. Employees were free to roam the city during their lunch hours, but management was adamant that no one leave the building during the two allotted fifteen-minute breaks. Like most rules, no one knew exactly why this one had been initiated. Fred considered it a particularly foolish injunction, and so he chose to ignore it. This was easy enough to do, since a fire exit door was next to his desk. He could slip out—being careful to insert a pencil between the door and the door frame—skip down the three flights of stairs to the ground floor street exit, and grab a doughnut and a cup of coffee from Mocha's on the corner.

A week after Fred's visit to Mr. Horn's office, I looked up in time to see Davidson scurrying back to his desk. Minutes later a loud banging attracted our attention, and we all watched as Mr. Horn marched solemnly across the office and opened the fire door. Fred, holding a cup of coffee, smiled ruefully.

This was a minor infraction—not in itself any job-jeopardizing event. But later that afternoon, as I made a pot of coffee, I looked back across the long room, across all those bowed, droning heads, and I saw Fred, wonderfully animate, leaning over Davidson's desk. The scene had many of the best qualities of classic silent films. The gestures were broad; emotions were clearly written on the faces of the participants, and action spoke as articulately as words. I watched Fred snatch a pencil off the desk and hold it up in front of Davidson's face. The caption here was "Do you recognize this?" Davidson backed away in the best tradition of villains, even throwing one arm across his chest, as though wielding a black cape. Fred leaned forward, grabbed Davidson by his shirt, and yanked him across the desk. Fred began hitting Davidson, wild, windmilling punches, and Davidson, rather than fight, curled up on the floor. Horn, Mrs. Alabaster, and a number of other employees came running. Davidson was moaning loudly, a sound so irritating that I confess to hoping Fred would quickly pummel him into unconsciousness.

The fight was broken up, and Fred was fired. He was, after all, the common denominator in two recent brawls.

I was sorry to see him go. Watching him clean his desk out was a sad business. He offered me a copy of *Playboy*, but I declined. In the following weeks, I met Fred once or twice for drinks. At these times he would vow to kill Davidson, but nothing came of it and one day he left to visit his brother in New Jersey. I never saw him again.

With reservations, I made the trip to Pennsylvania and spent Christmas with my family. We were all there: my younger brother, Joe, my older sister, Rachel, my parents, various uncles and aunts and cousins.

The holiday made me edgy and I was impatient to get back to my own apartment, my own simple routines. I suspect that I have a mild form of agoraphobia, since this desire to return to my apartment asserts itself on every vacation I've ever taken.

I drove home in a snowstorm. At times, I seemed to drive through a sheer, luminous whiteness, occasionally passing some car abandoned in a ditch. I felt oddly safe in my heated vehicle, oddly invulnerable as the windshield wipers thunked back and forth. I thought about the few conversations I had had with Sadie and the way she leaned forward and touched me when she talked and the way she used her eyebrows to convey a rich, erotic subtext. Reviewing these conversations, I thought it probable that she liked me, that something might very well develop if I asked her out. She never seemed all that excited about Webb, and there was every possibility that that romance was already on the rocks. The more I thought about it, the more likely it seemed. Webb had recently been looking sort of weepy and petulant and on more than one occasion I had seen him regarding his paramour, as she flirted with one or another of us office drones, with sunken eyes that contained either anger or despair, perhaps both. Now that I thought about it, I remembered Webb actually dragging Sadie away from—of all people to be jealous of!—the dour Davidson whom Sadie had been gaily pelting with rubber bands.

I was home in time to attend the New Year's Eve office party thrown annually by Mr. Colson, who owned a mansion in McLean. I hate parties, but I knew that Sadie would be there—without Webb. For once I had read the signs correctly. Sadie had dumped poor Webb, who had been so shaken and demoralized by this event that he had failed to come to work, had neglected even to call in, and, when reached on the phone by Mr. Horn, had sounded drunk and insisted that Horn put Sadie on the line. Horn had refused, words had been exchanged, and Webb no longer worked for Kimberly and Colson.

The time was ripe for me to make my move. He who hesitates is lost, et cetera.

The huge living room of the Colson mansion was decorated for the holidays. Colored balloons filled with helium covered the ceiling. A live rock band negotiated the current hits with some competence and a mass of brightly colored humanity danced and drank and declared their individual identities with loud speeches or simple hoots and shouts.

I spotted Sadie wearing a red outfit that lodged somewhere between elaborate fashion and an elf costume. A very short skirt displayed legs that might have been too Rubenesque for some tastes, but they seemed wildly beneficent to me. Accosted by so much flesh, I felt incapable of asking Sadie for a date. She was so blatantly sexual that asking her to attend a movie with me would—to anyone within hearing—sound like the crudest of propositions. That is how I saw it. Youth is acutely self-aware.

Sadie hugged me. I could smell a sweet, red scent of alcohol on her breath. It occurred to me that I could use a drink myself. I found the punch and returned to Sadie's side. Not surprisingly, several other males had chosen to locate themselves near her. Among these was the despised Davidson, who was holding the hand of a skinny girl with dull brown hair.

Davidson, who was looking ill at ease, saw me and smiled. Since I sat next to him at work, he saw me as a familiar face, even a comrade. It is a sad commentary on my reserve that I had never been able to convey to him how strongly I loathed him.

"Alec," he said, "this is my fiancée, Dorothy Cooms."

I took the limp and boneless hand of Miss Cooms, which was proffered in the manner of a socialite presenting a check to a welfare case.

"Nice to meet you," I said. She wore thick, tortoise-shell glasses and her hair was as limp as her handshake.

"We really should be going," Miss Cooms told Davidson.

"It's New Year's Eve," Davidson said. "We should at least stay until midnight. That's the purpose of these things, you know."

Just then Sadie grabbed Davidson and kissed him. "Yipes!" she shouted. "Fucking mistletoe."

Miss Cooms glared at Sadie. Sadie rushed about hugging other men. Suddenly Miss Cooms turned and marched away. Davidson started to follow her, then stopped. I watched his face shift under the weight of some resolve.

I did not leave the party until two in the morning and finally managed, just before leaving, to find Sadie alone. I had seen her head toward the bathroom and had waited in the hall for her return.

My courage reinforced by alcohol, I asked her if she would like to go to a movie sometime.

She smiled, seemed slightly surprised, but quickly recovered. She reached forward and pushed my hair out of my eyes. "Sure," she said. "I'd love to, Alec."

I left the party feeling wonderful, and I lay in bed in my apartment and said to the ceiling, "Sure. I'd love to, Alec." Like all shy people, it took little to excite me, and this seemed an extraordinary circumstance. I would savor these good feelings before actually asking her out. Being a pessimist, I assumed that a day would come when she would cease to like me, and I wanted to prolong this period of happiness and anticipation.

The period of bliss was even shorter than I anticipated. I awoke New Year's Day with the beginning of a bad cold. My throat ached and I felt feverish. I stayed in bed, feeling worse as the day progressed. Outside, snow fell steadily, large wet flakes that choked the window panes and rounded the world.

At noon the phone rang. A woman's voice asked to speak to Alfred Davidson.

"I'm sorry, he's not here," I said. "Who is this?"

The pause went on for so long that I thought the phone had gone dead, then: "This is Dorothy Cooms. Is this Alec Macphail?"

I admitted that that was indeed who she was talking to and that no, I hadn't seen her fiancé. She said this was very odd.

She said that she had left the party early. Davidson lived with his parents and didn't have a car. Miss Cooms had driven them to the party in her car, and when she had decided to leave early she had been unable to convince him to leave. "He wanted to see the New Year in, despite the pagan nature of such rituals," she said. So she left him, assuming he could secure a ride home from some fellow reveler.

This morning, repentant, Miss Cooms had called Davidson's house only to be told by Davidson's mother that the early morning snowstorm had taken everyone by surprise and that her son had called from the party to say he was staying the night at a friend's apartment rather than negotiate treacherous roads.

Dorothy Cooms had found my home number in the employee's handbook and thought I might be the referred-to friend. I said that I was not. She asked if I could suggest anyone. I couldn't.

My cold progressed, and I called in sick the following day. I lay in bed reading the Edgar Rice Burroughs Martian books and ministering to myself with aspirin, ginger ale, and chicken soup. I thought about Alfred Davidson and where he had been when he had not returned to his parents' home. My thoughts led dismally to Sadie Thompson, whose apartment was somewhere in Alexandria and whose roommate was—if I remembered correctly—away visiting her parents in Tampa, Florida.

The afternoon of my first day back at work, I encountered

Davidson in the restroom. He confirmed my worst fears. "I've got to talk to someone," he said, clutching me as though he were drowning.

I said nothing, but regarded him through narrowed eyes. He was disheveled and red-eyed and his long, bony fingers dug into my arms with obscene strength.

"I lied to Dorothy. I know she called you . . ." His voice trickled away. And then, suddenly, he wailed, a ghastly sound that bounced off the cinderblock walls and echoed through the stalls.

"I'm a sinner!" he shouted. "I am a miserable, lost sinner! I have given in to lust and temptation. No, I have sought it out. I have wallowed in it and rejoiced in my depravity. Sin. Blackest sin! I am a miserable sinner."

He was beginning to repeat himself, and I felt overwhelmed with disgust. Tears were streaming down his cheeks, and his whole countenance seemed to be losing definition, melting.

I shoved him away from me and he bounced against the wall. He slid slowly down the wall and into a sitting position, still sobbing. I turned and walked out of the restroom.

Sadie seemed much the same that day, as untouched as ever. I watched her flirt with old man Rainey, and a smooth, cold anger filled me.

Davidson did not return to his desk. Mr. Horn came by and said that Davidson had gone home ill and would I mind checking to see if there was anything pressing on his desk?

Later Sadie stopped at my desk. "What about that movie?" she said.

I didn't say anything. I was thinking of her locked in Davidson's clammy embrace.

"Hello in there," Sadie said, leaning forward. Her hair brushed my face.

"When are you going to take me to that movie?" she asked.

"Perhaps Davidson should take you," I said. The words surprised me but I didn't take them back.

Sadie pulled away from me and regarded me coolly. "Oh yeah. Me and Davidson. Fucking speed-of-light gossip. Keep me posted, Alec."

She turned and marched away. She was fiercely seductive in her retreat. I yearned to apologize but my self-righteousness would not allow it. The other men had been different. It was her *taste* I now despised.

When I arrived home that evening, I found Davidson waiting outside my apartment, hugging himself in the cold, flapping his arms like an earthbound crow.

I walked past him and unlocked my door.

"I've got to talk to you," he said.

I let him come inside. He sat down on the sofa and put his face in his hands. Without looking up, he said, "It would be a Christian thing to help me. You could tell Dorothy that I stayed here."

"I already told her you weren't here," I said, going to the refrigerator and getting a beer. I didn't offer Davidson one. I assumed he didn't drink—his principles would forbid it. Anyway, I didn't want to do anything to prolong his visit.

Davidson lifted his face from his hands. "It was the drink that made me do it. I drank some of the punch. I pretended I didn't know it was alcoholic. I knew of course. And when Sadie said I could stay at her place, I accepted, knowing I would . . . I would . . . I was aware of her reputation."

"I don't want to hear it," I said.

Davidson stood up. "I kissed her. But it was the inflamed lust of alcohol. I would have . . . I'll say it . . . I would have thrust my tongue in her mouth had she not prevented me."

171

Here Davidson sank back onto the sofa, moaning. "Sinner. Gosh darned no good black-hearted sinner! Dorothy will kill me."

I stood there blinking at Davidson as he rocked on the sofa, sobbing and going on about sin and damnation.

"Are you saying all you did was kiss her?"

Davidson rocked on, sobbing.

I reached down and shook him. He looked up. Again, his face was blurred, his eyes red. "Sinner," he sobbed. "Oh I would have done more had she let me. There were no limits, no shame to my lust."

I have never felt a rage come over me like the one that came over me at the moment. Much of my anger was, I realize now, self-disgust. I began to hit Davidson. He slid off the sofa and I began to kick him. He stumbled to the door. "You son of a bitch!" I was shouting.

"You don't know what sin is!" I screamed (which, even at the time, seemed the words of some third party shouted over my shoulder).

I suppose my usual reserve had abandoned me. I watched Davidson run down the sidewalk, slip, pick himself up and start running again. I prayed he would fall and break his neck.

The next day I tried to apologize to Sadie. I waited for her break and then asked her if she would come out in the hall.

"No thanks," she said.

"Please. I've got to talk to you."

Grudgingly, she agreed. "Let's hear it."

I realized then that I didn't know what to say. "I'm sorry," I said.

"Yeah? For what?"

I shrugged my shoulders. "Well, for what I said. I mean . . . about Davidson and you . . ."

Sadie leaned toward me. She never had much fear of invading another's space. She placed a palm flat on my chest. "You're a fucking Shakespeare with the fucking words," she said. "I know what you thought. Me and the Reverend Davidson banging ourselves blue . . . that's what you thought, huh?"

Again, I could do nothing but look stupid and remorseful. Words eluded me.

"Well, I'll tell you something," Sadie said, in what were to be the last words she ever spoke to me, "I don't have too fucking high an opinion of you either, Alec Macphail. In fact, I think you are a fucking pig. That's "P" fucking "I" fucking "G.""

"I can understand that," I said.

In the interests of literary conservation, a number of the characters in the above story have been recycled from Somerset Maugham's classic "Rain." We live on a small planet, and it is time we stopped the profligate creation of new characters and used the perfectly viable ones that already exist.

—The Author

A Child's Christmas In Florida

The week before Christmas, Luke Haliday killed the tradi-
tional mud turtle, gutted it, and gave its shell to his oldest
son, Hark. Hark painted the shell with day-glo colors and
wore it on his head, where it would remain until two days
before Christmas when the youngest of the children, Lou
Belle, would snatch it from his head, run giggling down to
the creek, and fill the gaudy shell with round, smooth stones.

"I miss Harrisburg," Janice Mosely said to her husband.
"It should be cold at Christmas. There should be snow."
Her husband didn't say anything, but simply leaned over his
newspaper like he might dive into it. Well, Al could ignore
her if he pleased. She knew he missed Pennsylvania too and
just didn't care to talk about it. There was no getting around
it: Christmas was for colder climes, everyone all bundled up
and hustling from house to house with presents, red-faced
children, loud, wet people in the hall peeling off layers of
clothing, scarves, boots, gloves, shouting because they were
full of hot life that winter had failed to freeze and ready for
any marvelous thing. And snow, snow could make the world
look like the cellophane had just been shucked from it, was
still crackling in the air.

"Barbara says it snowed eight inches last week," Janice
said. Barbara was their daughter. Al Mosely looked up from

his newspaper and regarded his wife with pale, sleepy blue eyes. A wispy cloud of gray hair bloomed over his high forehead, giving his face a truculent, just-wakened cast. In fact, he had been up since five (his unvarying routine) and regarded his wife's nine o'clock appearance at the breakfast table as something approaching decadence.

"She'll have to get that dodger"—Al always referred to Barbara's live-in boyfriend as "that dodger," an allusion to the young man's ability to avoid matrimony—"She'll have to get that dodger to shovel her walk this year," Al said. "She was the one who was so hot for us to retire to Florida, and we done it and we'll just see if she gets that layabout to do anything more than wait for the spring thaw."

"Oh Al," Janice said, waving a hand at him and turning away. She walked into the living room and stared out the window. Not only had they moved to Florida, they had moved to rural Florida, land of cows and scrub pines and cattle egrets. Her husband had said, "Okay, I'll go to Florida, but not to some condominium on the ocean. I don't want a place full of old folks playing bridge and shuffleboard. If I'm gonna retire, I'm gonna retire right. A little place in the country—that's the ticket."

Janice watched a yellow dog walk out into the road. Its image shimmered in the heat, like a bad television transmission. Christmas. Christmas in Loomis, Florida. Dear God. Why, none of her neighbors had even put up lights. And maybe they had the right idea. Why bother? There was no way this flat, sandy place could cobble up a Christmas to fool a half-wit.

As Janice Mosely stared out the window, three boys, the tallest of them wearing a funny, brightly colored beanie, marched by. A tiny little girl ran in their wake. The boys were carrying a Christmas tree. With an air of triumphant

176

high spirits, they wrestled it down the road, shouting to each other, country boys in tattered jeans and t-shirts and home-cropped haircuts, boys full of reckless enthusiasm and native rudeness. Janice smiled and scolded herself. "Well, it's a perfectly fine Christmas for some, Mrs. Janice 'Scrooge' Mosely," she said out loud. Still smiling, she turned away from the window and walked back into the kitchen. Her husband was listening to the radio, the news, all of it bleak: war, famine, murder, political graft.

"What's the world coming to?" Janice asked her husband.

"Let me think about it before I answer," Al said.

Hark was the oldest boy, but he wasn't right in the head, so Danny, who was three years younger, was in charge. "You don't do it that way," Danny said. "You will just bust your fingers doing it that way. Boy, you are a rattlebrain."

"Shut up," Hark said. "If you know what's good for you, shut up."

"What's the problem here?" their father asked, coming into the backyard. Luke Haliday was a tall, lanky man with a bristly black mustache. There wasn't any nonsense in him and his children knew it. He had been very strict since their mother left. Now he said, "Maybe you would rather fight than have a Christmas?"

"No, no!" shouted little Lou Belle who was so infused with the spirit of Christmas that it made her eyes bulge. The boys, Hark, Danny, and Calder, all shouted: "No, no."

"I was just trying to explain to Hark that you got to tie these traps onto the tree first and then set em. You do it the other way, you just catch all your fingers," Danny said.

Luke laid a hand on Hark's shoulder. "Is this the first tree you ever decorated?" he asked his son.

"No sir," Hark said.

"Well then," Luke said.

"Tie em, then set em," Hark said, kicking dirt.

Luke stood back from his children and regarded the Christmas tree; the boys had dug a hole for the trunk and braced it with wires and stakes. The tree stood straight, tall and proud, the field rolling out behind it. "That's a damned fine tree," Luke said. "You children got an eye for a tree. You take this one out of Griper's field?"

"Yes sir," Danny said.

"It's a good one," their father said. He reached down, picked up one of the mousetraps, and tied it to a branch with a piece of brown string. Then he set the trap and stood back again. The tree already had a dozen traps tied to various branches. "If a tree like this can't bring us luck then we might as well give up. We might as well lie down and let them skin us and salt us if a tree like this don't bode a fine Christmas."

The children agreed.

Their father turned and walked back to the shack, and the children set to work tying the remaining traps to branches. Later they would paint colored dots on them. "I want blue," Lou Belle insisted. "I want mine blue." Her voice was shrill, prepared for an argument, but Danny just said, "Sure. Why not?"

"Hello," Janice shouted, when she saw the little girl again. "Hello, little girl." The child turned and stared at Janice for a long time before finally changing course and toddling toward the old woman.

"Lou Belle," the little girl said in answer to Janice's question. *What a sweet child*, Janice thought, with such full cheeks—they cried out to be pinched—and those glorious, big brown eyes. The girl wore corduroy overalls and a white t-shirt. Her feet were bare.

"What's Santa bringing you for Christmas?" Janice asked.

The girl shrugged her shoulders. "Santa don't come to our house," she said.

"Oh, I'm sure he does." Janice knelt down and placed her hands on the child's shoulders. Lou Belle was a frail little thing. "Santa wouldn't miss a sweet little girl like you."

"Yes'm," the girl said. "He don't come anymore. He left. He and my mommy. They went to live in sin."

"Goodness," Janice said. What an odd child.

Janice stood up. "Would you like to see my Christmas tree? I just finished decorating it, and I thought, 'There's no one around to see it except Al'—that's my husband, and he couldn't care less about such things. And then I looked out the window and there you were, and I thought, 'I bet that little girl would like to see this tree.'"

"Yes'm," Lou Belle said, and she followed Janice Mosely into the house, and she studied the evergreen that Janice had harried her husband into buying and which she had then decorated carefully, all the while listening to Christmas music and ignoring her husband's grumblings and general humbuggery.

Lou Belle touched the glass ornaments. Lou Belle leaned close and blinked at the hand-sewn angels. She even rubbed the styrofoam snowman against her cheek—it made a *skritch, skritch* sound—but finally she stepped back and said, "It won't catch nuthin."

Lou Belle thought about it that night when she couldn't sleep. Silly old lady. What could you catch inside a house, anyway? Even with the best of traps?

Lou Belle couldn't sleep because tomorrow was Omen Day, the third day before Christmas. Last night they had baited the traps, and this morning they would get out of bed while it was still dark out; they would wake their father and he would make them eat breakfast first, while they craned their necks and peered out the back window, trying to squint through the darkness. Father would move slow, especially slow out of that meanness that adults have, and he would fix eggs and toast and talk about everything, as though it weren't Omen Day at all but any normal day and finally, finally, when they had all finished and were watching and fidgeting as their father mopped up the last of his eggs with a bread crust, he would say, "All right, let's see what we've got."

And it would still be dark, and he would grab up the big lantern flashlight and they would run down to the tree.

Who could possibly sleep the night before Omen Day?

And when it finally did come, when Lou Belle could stand it no longer and ran into her brother Hark's room and woke him and then the two of them fetched Danny and Calder and the long, long breakfast was endured, they pushed the screen door open and ran out into the darkness of the yard. Her heart thrummed like a telephone wire in a hurricane. The grass was wet under her feet.

She thought she would faint when her father, moving the flashlight over the tree, said, "There's a lizard. That's a red dot. Calder, that's you." She wanted to cry out, "No! Not Calder! I'm the Chosen!" But before she could scream, her father spoke again, in a low, awed whisper. "Well, would you look at that." And Lou Belle followed the flashlight's beam with her eyes, and there, flapping awkwardly, caught, like a wound-down toy, was a black, furry lump, and her breathing flipped backwards and she said, in a hiccup of triumph, "Bat!" And she knew, before her father called out "Blue, that's Lou Belle" that it was hers.

And she didn't need her father to tell her that bat was best, that bat was the king of good luck. She clapped her hands and laughed.

"Light the tree, Lou Belle," they urged her, and she

smelled the kerosene smell that was, more than anything, the smell of Christmas, and her father gave her the burning straw and she thrust it forward, and the whole tree stood up with flame, *whoosh*, and in the brightness she could see the bat, her bat, and she squealed with joy. Then her father started it off, with his fine, deep voice. "Silent night, holy night," he sang. They all joined in. "All is calm, all is bright."

"Listen," Janice said to her husband. "Do you hear that?"

"What?"

"Carolers," Janice said. "Isn't that nice?"

Because Lou Belle was the Chosen, she stole the mud turtle shell from Hark and filled it with smooth stones. And on Christmas Eve, just before twilight, Lou Belle distributed the stones among her brothers, and they each made their wishes on them and solemnly threw them into the lake, and then they all climbed into the back of their father's pickup truck and drove into town and on past the town and down to Clearwater and late, very late at night, with the salt air filling her lungs, Lou Belle fell asleep, her head resting on a dirty blanket smelling faintly of gasoline. When she woke it was dark, thick, muggy dark, and Hark was urging her out of the truck. She ran after them, instantly alert. A bouncing, silver ball on the grass was the orb of her father's flashlight.

They were in a suburb. She heard glass break and then Danny was beside her. "Come on, come on," he was whispering.

Oh. Her father had pushed open the sliding glass door to reveal, like a magician, a treasure of gifts, gaudily wrapped boxes, all strewn under a thick-bodied Christmas tree pinpricked with yellow lights. Amid all the gift-wrapped boxes, a marvelous orange tricycle with yellow handlebars glowed.

"Oh," Lou Belle said. She pointed a stubby finger at the

bike, and her father moved swiftly across the room, lifted the bike and returned to her.

"Shhhhhhhhhhh," her father said, raising a finger to his lips.

Hark and Danny and Calder were busy under the tree. Calder raised both hands, clutching a brand new air rifle, a smile scrawled across his face.

This is the best Christmas, the best, Lou Belle thought. Next year some of the magic would be gone. Other Christmases would bring disillusionment. She would learn, as her brothers already knew, that her father took great pains to discover a proper house, and that it was his vigilance and care in the choosing that was important, not the catch on Omen Day, not how fervently the wishes were placed on the turtle stones.

But for now it was all magic, and as they raced back across the lawn and piled into the truck, as the motor caught with a sound like thunder, as someone behind them shouted, Lou Belle sent a quick prayer to the baby Jesus, king of thieves.

Best Man

I had been married for five years when Harry Bream showed up on my doorstep. I hadn't seen him in all that time. I think he was wearing the same suit, a wrinkled, gravy-colored polyester. The suit was large but not large enough, Harry being three hundred and fifty pounds of opinionated fat man. A tailor would have winced, imagining the sound of ripping seams.

Behind Harry, the grey December sky bellied out with the weight of incipient snow, like the sprung ceiling of some condemned tenement. Harry could make any landscape— even this ordered, suburban one—seem seedy and faintly surreal.

"Does Joyce still hate me?" Harry asked, standing there in the cold.

"I think so," I said.

"Is she here?"

I told him that my wife was still at work, would be home in about an hour. I'd left work at noon, thanks to my friend Doug. We had been horsing around at the water cooler, and he had sucker punched me in the stomach. It wasn't anything serious, but it had dampened my enthusiasm for the office, and I had driven home, hunched over the wheel like a bilious Quasimodo.

Now here was Harry at my door. "I've come to say I'm

sorry, Dennis. I've come to apologize," Harry said, sliding into the foyer and moving swiftly down the hall to the kitchen, where he opened the refrigerator door. "These Miller Lites all you got?" he shouted. He had pulled the four beers out and was holding them by an empty plastic loop.

"I wasn't expecting company," I said.

Harry came back into the living room, the beer cans dangling from his fist like a string of fish. He sank into the sofa.

"It's okay," he said, the beers settling in his lap. "I should watch my weight anyway."

He popped a beer, it fizzed up, and he ducked his head to suck the foaming brew.

"You think I got a chance of making up with Joyce?" he asked, wiping his mouth with the back of his hand. He seemed suddenly fragile, childlike. Beneath the fuzzy, brillo-pad beard, chins were trembling.

"I don't know," I said, "You killed her brother, you know. And on her wedding day, too."

I had been standing up, but now I sat in the big armchair, facing Harry, and I leaned forward. "I won't lie and say they were close, but a woman is a nervous wreck on her wedding day, and when the best man shoots the bride's brother, who is also an usher, hard feelings are bound to arise. You just naturally want things to go smoothly on your wedding day. I don't mind telling you that I am not one hundred per cent resentment-free myself. I have mixed feelings about your reappearance."

"It was an accident," Harry grumbled, "and it was five years ago. And it's not like I ruined the wedding. I didn't shoot Justin until after the ceremony."

"You ruined the reception, that's for sure. And maybe it was five years ago, but time doesn't heal everything," I said. "Some things just set, like cement. Anyway, what brings you back now?"

"I'm having a mid-life crisis," Harry said. "I figured I needed to patch things up."

He lay back on my sofa, slipped his shoes off, and swung his feet up. He crushed the first beer can, set it on the end table, and found a second one.

Staring at the ceiling, he told me what he had been doing since I last saw him. He said that after the unpleasantness of the coroner's hearing, he couldn't stay in town. He drifted all over the U.S. Taught at this girls' college for awhile. Bartended some. Wrote an advice column for a Midwestern newspaper. Bummed around the Northwest. Got a job as a park ranger in King's Canyon.

Harry looked at me and raised his eyebrows. "One day I said to myself, 'It's time, Harry,' and here I am."

"I don't know," I said.

"It's got to be time sometime," he said.

Watching Harry lying there on the sofa, drinking my beers, I felt the smarmy embrace of nostalgia. Old Harry. We had been best friends in college. Even then, he was a moody kind of a guy, something of a slob, and an incredible moocher. We never roomed together, but when he visited my apartment, he would drink all my beers and eat everything in my fridge. He even brushed his teeth with my toothbrush which was pretty gross behavior, and still, I liked him. I liked his intensity. He was a philosophy major, and he took life seriously. He was a man of strong, loud opinions.

When we first met—in a bar called *The Burnt Orange*—he told me that he was studying philosophy to discover whether or not he should go on living. He was serious about this. "I hate Hamlet. That dirty waffler. Someone should have wrung his neck."

Harry believed that the study of philosophy would either kill him or cure him, either plunge him into suicidal despair or offer some solid reasons for going on.

Well, Harry hadn't killed himself (thanks, he said, to Spinoza), but he *had* killed Joyce's brother, Justin. In 1987, Harry had been sitting in my father-in-law's study with Justin Rhodes. Justin and Harry were drinking champagne and congratulating themselves on being single. The mansion grounds had just been the setting for my wedding to Joyce. Harry had performed best man honors and Justin had ushered.

They were hiding out in the study and reflecting—as men will at weddings and funerals—on the fine line separating the quick from the dead.

And then, life never tiring of irony, Harry had admired the deer rifle on a rack behind Justin's head, and Justin had said, "It's a beauty all right; here, have a look at it," and Justin had reached back and lifted it off its rack and handed it to Harry; and Harry had immediately taken the rifle and shot Justin through the heart and run, screaming, out into the cool April twilight, sending a great crowd of overdressed guests into panic and causing my new bride to faint in my arms.

It had been an accident—the clichéd tragedy of the gun that was not supposed to be loaded—and the inquest came to the same conclusion. But accident or no accident, Joyce wasn't eager to see Harry, and I felt a certain diffidence myself. Then Harry left for parts unknown.

Now he was back and lying on my sofa, primed for reconciliation. "Let's say, for argument's sake, that Joyce still hates me. I mean, she was never crazy about me, okay. I don't think she likes fat people as a group because she fears becoming fat herself and sees us as the enemy. But I think I can convince her, logically, that her anger is irrational."

"Harry," I said, "Don't get your hopes up. You know Joyce can be stubborn."

Harry crushed the second beer and opened a third one. "Well, it's been nagging at me. I can't get any rest until I've tried. Five years I've been drifting around the country, never able to settle, and I had this insight: I won't ever be at peace until Joyce forgives me."

"Well—" I began. Just then I heard the door open, and apparently Harry heard it too, because he swung his feet off the sofa and sat upright.

Joyce came into the room. She is a small, thin woman with no fashion sense, and she was wearing extremely large round glasses and a grey suit that emitted an air of profound censure. She was lugging a briefcase large enough for shoplifting VCRs. With her frizzled, yellow hair, her magnified eyes, and her general awkwardness, she resembled a child playing daddy-comes-home-from-the-office. A draft of cold air blew in with her, and I jumped up and hugged her.

"Look who's here," I said.

Joyce has never liked any of my friends. Not, in any event, those friends that I had before I met her. She may be jealous of them—no doubt that explains the animosity that exists between many a new wife and her husband's longtime friends. But I think, to do Joyce justice, that she is incapable of liking my friends because, by and large, they are unlikable.

To list just a few of my old friends and their rough edges:

Bob Hapsburg. Cannot be interrupted. Talks only about illnesses he has had or expects to have. Is eloquent but repetitive about his digestive system.

Darrel Lodge. A very thin man generally sporting some variety of food in a large, yarn-like mustache. Always talks in the plural, being married to a woman who fascinates him. Darrel was my roommate my sophomore year in college. Joyce has never met his wife, but she has heard that wife's every opinion and finds her insufferably long-winded. Joyce tells me she hates the ghostly Mrs. Lodge more than the wan presence of her Boswell-like husband.

John Lepholdt. A long-haired, wired individual who believes that his life is in jeopardy because of what he knows about the JFK and Hoffa assassinations. On more than one occasion he has sought refuge at my house at two or three in the morning. I assure Joyce that he is harmless, but even I have to admit that he seems a little less coherent, a little more fragmented, with each passing year. His heart is in the right place, though, and he has offered to give me a tidy sum when he decodes the Mafia-run Maryland lottery (the secret of which is lodged in the 1979 Dayton, Ohio phone book).

But enough. I merely wished to demonstrate that I have acquired the sort of friends that *any* wife might dislike, and that Joyce is not unreasonably intolerant. "Did you seek these people out?" she always asks me, and on days when my old friends are trying my patience, I wonder if I am unique in the number of friends I have that would be of interest to a clinical psychologist. Suffice it to say, that on the day of my wedding, Harry Bream was the most solid of the lot, and that's how he landed the position of best man.

I've digressed, however—and at a critical juncture.

Joyce turned and glared at me. "Dennis," she said. "How could you?"

"What?" I said.

"You know what," she said. "What is he doing here?"

Harry is not much in the nuance department, but I could see that he was uncomfortable. Somewhere along the line he had learned that when a friend's spouse refers to you in the third person she is manifesting some coolness.

Harry stood up. "Joyce, I've come to make my apologies!"

"Get out!" Joyce screamed.

"Let bygones be bygones," he said.

"How dare you come here!" Joyce shouted. "How dare—"

That's when Harry produced the gun. It was a small, black revolver, and he pulled it out of his pocket.

"Look," he said. Joyce stepped backward, dropping her briefcase, and Harry was suddenly at her side. He had slapped the gun into her palm and returned to the sofa before I could move from the armchair.

"Shoot me," he said.

Joyce was staring in horror at the gun in her hand. My Joyce hates all forms of violence, and even refuses to watch old episodes of "I Love Lucy" for what she sees as a sort of slapstick vandalism that should not be condoned or endured.

"Shoot me," Harry said. "I deserve it. You know I do."

I watched my wife's eyes narrow behind those shiny, round glasses. I believe if my friend Jack Besler hadn't visited me from Kansas City the week before, everything would still have been okay. But Jack had come, accompanied by his girlfriend Sally, and they had run naked through our house, snapping each other with towels, giggling wildly, creating a mountain of dirty dishes and empty pizza cartons.

Sally had accused Joyce of being "an uptight juiceless office Jane" which, Sally said, was an observation, not an attack, but Joyce had been offended, I could see that.

I really think that if Harry's timing had been different, if he hadn't arrived right on the heels of Jack and Sally, things might have been different.

"What's the deal?" Joyce said, an unusual, metallic glitter in her half-closed eyes.

"Shoot me," Harry said. "I don't expect you to just say everything's okay. I understand that something real is required. An eye for an eye, Joyce. So shoot me."

"Is this thing loaded?" Joyce said, eyeing the gun with a reflective air.

Harry smiled. "Oh yes. There's only one real bullet though. That's the beauty of it. The rest are blanks or duds. Every time you pull that trigger, Joyce, there is the very real chance that you'll kill me. Maybe you will, maybe you won't. Even I don't know where the real bullet is. It might be at the top. First pull of the trigger and 'Bang!' I'm dead. Or it might be the last bullet. Each time you pull that trigger, you can think about it. Just how much do you hate me, Joyce? Just how much?"

Joyce answered by pulling the trigger. *Click!*—a small, hard noise that filled up the room. She smiled. Harry sat with a beer on his lap. Beads of sweat steamed on his forehead. He looked scared now. She pulled the trigger again. *Click.*

"Joyce," I said. "Joyce, honey."

Bang! Harry's beer flew into the air, and he flopped backwards, arms outstretched. He rolled right off the sofa, taking a lamp with him. The end table overturned.

"Jesus!" I screamed. I ran to Harry. He lay on his back, arms flung out. He was bleeding. There was blood on his head. But then he opened his eyes and smiled. He stood up.

Joyce was shaking, the gun pointed at the floor.

"You don't hate me anymore, do you?" Harry said. "That was just a blank, but you could have killed me. I know just how you felt when you saw me there. It's rotten, isn't it? But you didn't have to do it, see? I'll never escape, but you can. You see?"

Harry walked to Joyce and rested a hand on her shoulder.

"You don't want to shoot me, do you?" he asked.

She shook her head no, not looking at him, staring instead at the floor. Harry kissed her on the cheek and walked past her and out the door.

"Honey," I said, going to her. "You okay?" I led her to the sofa. "That Harry's something, isn't he?"

I sank back in the armchair. "He got my adrenalin flowing, I'll tell you that. I mean, what was that crazy stunt supposed to prove? What? You tell me."

I smiled, the sad, reconciliatory smile of a husband who is aware that his friends are a trying lot.

Joyce smiled back and pointed the gun at me.

"Ha ha," I said, "Very funny."

Click!

"Hey," I shouted, "Cut it out. Harry might not have been kidding. There might be a live bullet in there. I wouldn't put it past him."

Click! She was now holding the gun with both hands, and her smile had enlarged. Her eyes were hard to see behind the highlights of her glasses.

"Not funny," I said. "You're acting crazy."

Joyce giggled.

I didn't like the sound—not one bit.

Daughter Doom

"Mother," Gloria said at breakfast, "I believe there is something wrong with my knees."

Gloria's mother, Gail Hermans, buttered her toast, and said, "Indeed?"

"Oh yes." Gloria leaned across the table and touched her mother's arm. "You'll remember this conversation later and say, 'I wish I had paid more attention to my daughter when she spoke of her knees. If we'd only caught it in time . . .' That sort of thing."

"Well, what about your knees?" said Mrs. Hermans, taking a small bite from her toast and brushing crumbs from the newspaper spread out before her. "Are you feeling an odd numbness in them? Are there small needles of pain just under the skin? Are they hot? Are they cold? Do they feel— let's see—as though someone were breathing on them? Are they making noises, squeaking perhaps like rusty hinges?"

Gloria brushed her jet black hair back, frowned, sat up straight in her chair, and replied, in her coolest voice, "Your words will burn like red-hot pokers when I'm dead and gone, Mother. I want you to know, right now, that I forgive you."

"That's a comfort," said Mrs. Hermans. "But I am listening, Gloria. Please proceed."

Gail Hermans and her daughter looked much alike, sitting

193

across the table in the small breakfast room, crisp fall sunlight illuminating their pale faces. They both possessed large brown eyes, delicate, heart-stopping eyebrows, and fine, imperious cheekbones. Mrs. Hermans—with a charity luncheon to attend—was already dressed elegantly, her small diamond earrings full of bright assurance. Gloria was in a blue bathrobe, her nine-year-old body whippet-thin and brittle with indignation.

"Well," said Gloria, learning forward. "I don't know the medical term for it of course." Gloria frowned again. "I don't know where our *Merck Manual* is these days. I suspect it's been thrown out. Anyway, what seems to have happened is that my kneecaps have become detached, somehow, and actually, well, move. I can push them about with my fingers." Gloria stopped and studied her mother, who was smiling. "Well?" Gloria said, with some vehemence. "Well?"

Mrs. Hermans sighed. "Gloria, that's perfectly natural."

Gloria snorted her disdain, "Mother, you are not a doctor, are you?"

Mrs. Hermans paused, as though trying to remember if she had, in fact, acquired a medical degree at some point in her life. "No, I'm not a doctor, but I have kneecaps of my own, and if I were a morbid person, I could sit around all day and push them around. It is the nature of kneecaps to be somewhat mobile."

"Oh Mother," Gloria said, throwing her napkin down on her plate, "you are no comfort. All you're saying is that it's genetic. I've inherited it from you. That's great, just great." And Gloria jumped up and left the table.

Mrs. Hermans shouted after her daughter. "The bus will be here in twenty minutes, honey. Don't dawdle. And please, dear, no sunglasses in class. I don't want to talk to Mrs. Childress again; that woman and I are on different wavelengths."

On the bus, Rod Markley sat next to her. "How come you always wear sunglasses?" he wanted to know. He was a blond, fat boy with freckles.

"I'm not supposed to look directly at people without them on," Gloria said. "My doctor says my eyes are too strong. If I look at someone, they might get leukemia. Do you know what leukemia is?"

Rod Markley narrowed his eyes and said nothing.

"It's when your blood dies," Gloria said. "It's rotten. It feels like there are hundreds of spiders in your veins."

"That's not true," Rod Markley said.

Gloria whipped her glasses off and leaned over, staring into the fat boy's blue eyes. Gloria spoke in a detached, clinical voice: "Do you feel any itching on the inside of your eyes? Or do you feel as though your brain were floating in cold water?"

Rod Markley pushed her away and stood up. "You're crazy," he said, and he marched off to the back of the bus.

Gloria went into a trance when Mrs. Childress began talking about the Industrial Revolution. Mrs. Childress was always boring, but when she talked about the Industrial Revolution, she was so powerfully dull that it hypnotized Gloria.

"I can't feel my hands," Gloria thought, and the next thing she knew it was lunch.

After lunch they all watched a long movie about democracy and it was even more powerfully boring than the Industrial Revolution. Gloria amused herself by pretending she had died at her desk. Once dead, you could not move, so the way her head lay against the desktop, squashing her left arm, had to be endured. Death, she realized, might be remarkably uncomfortable. Or worse. She thought about the time Tim Wesley, a weak-minded, over-large boy, fished the dead turtle out of the creek and carried it around by its tail.

Being dead, it had had to endure all sorts of indignities without protest. Death, Gloria realized, was not being able to make a fuss.

While Gloria was thinking of death, her mother, older and more philosophically advanced, was thinking of God. "What," she asked Father Macomb, "keeps God from despairing?" Father Macomb, who was in the process of tugging on his pants, leaned back in the bed and planted a kiss on Gail Hermans' forehead. "Why *love*, Mrs. Hermans, flat-footed, hot-blooded, holy-roaring love."

Gail Hermans lay back on the bed and studied the ceiling. "I wouldn't think love was much of a match for eternity."

"Spoken like a true lost soul, my dear." Father Macomb said as he patted her hip. He smiled his roguish, pulpit-swooning smile.

When Gloria was seventeen, Allen Stevens told her he would die for her. He was an earnest young man with red lips and two deep creases between his eyebrows.

Gloria told young Stevens that there was no need for him to kill himself to prove his love for her. All she required was the first joint of his little finger—the left hand would do. If he would cut it off, she would know his love was true, and she would abandon all reticence and be his completely in body and soul.

"Hah hah," said Allen Stevens, straightening his tie.

"I'm not asking much," Gloria replied, in a tone that suggested she was not joking. "You offer me your life, and I am willing to settle for a mere sliver of flesh. And yet you seem to hesitate. Really, Allen, I think you have been toying with my affections. I am coming to doubt your sincerity."

Allen Stevens did not become Gloria's lover, and later in life, remembering how Gloria had looked that evening, virginal and radiant under an autumn moon, he would study his little finger with something like disgust before taking the trash out and settling down to a solitary dinner.

"I once had an affair with a priest," Mrs. Hermans said to her psychiatrist. The psychiatrist tapped a cigarette out of the pack on the nightstand and sat up in bed.

"Really," he said. "I had no idea you were religious."

Gail Hermans plucked the cigarette from her lover's lips and took a long drag. "I think having children makes one think in spiritual terms. I may not have a soul, but I'm certain Gloria has one. I only have to look into her eyes, and I see it moving about."

"This is the love of mothers," Dr. Geis said.

"I hope I'm not paying you for that sort of insight," Gail Hermans said.

The doctor assured her that he had ceased billing her long ago.

When Gloria was eighteen, she fell in love with a self-destructive young man named Bobby Winston who was a freshman at the college Gloria attended.

Bobby Winston wrote poetry that went like this:
"Death is a ziplock bag
full of worms
in a dirty refrigerator
in a crack-house
about to be raided."

"My mother worries about growing old," Gloria told him.

"Yeah, it's a thing with old dudes, growing old," said Winston. They had just made love, and he was bleeding a bit from the loss of his thumb, despite the layers of gauze.

Gloria sighed. "Yeah. I told her not to worry. You are either dead or alive, that's all. What are wrinkles? I mean, human beings are pretty flimsy things and yet they go on and on, really. I mean, think about eyes, for instance. They are sort of like grapes—and nobody expects a grape to last eighty years. One little slip with a sharp object and that's it, but people act like they are untouchable."

"People are weird," Bobby Winston said. He put the spoon under the flame and leaned forward. He drew the clear fluid into the syringe with great care. "They don't know what a crapshoot it is," he said.

Gloria agreed and snuggled close. She was holding him close when he died, when the bad dope vandalized his breath. Gloria woke—alerted by cold, unresponsive flesh—and finding him dead, she held him tighter and tried to sleep again. She dreamed.

She dreamed that she was crawling through a tunnel, a tunnel that smelled of rancid earth and blistering heat. The tunnel grew smaller as she wriggled forward on her stomach pursuing some small, pale sun in front of her. And then something caught her legs, and she peered down and saw her father's ancient face—for he had always been ancient, a mummy in a bed, unshaven, mired in plastic tubing, there in the back bedroom where the nurses lived—and he was trying to speak, but his tongue, purple and oddly animated, as though it were the carapace of—why, yes—a dead, a drowned, turtle, his tongue could form no words. And then, up ahead, she heard her mother's voice, saying, "Just take the pillow, darling. Just cover him with the pillow."

Mrs. Hermans lay on the couch. "Did I ever tell you I killed my husband?" she asked.

"Many times," the psychiatrist said.

Mrs. Hermans sighed. "I'm a broken record, I suppose. You know, my last psychiatrist, Dr. Geis, refused to believe me."

Dr. Morris smiled. "You sleep with a man, he is naturally less inclined to believe anything you say. I see no reason to doubt you, Gail. Your guilt is genuine. As far as I'm concerned, it is your guilt that validates your statement."

"I smothered him with a pillow. I only wish . . . I wish . . ."

Dr. Morris nodded. "You wish your daughter had not seen."

"Do you suppose she remembers? She was only three."

Dr. Morris leaned forward. "I think we remember everything," the old man said. "It's not the remembering that's critical; it's how we assimilate it."

Gloria was aware of the dawn; the darkness had drained away leaving a cold, gritty ache. She lay on her side. She was not fully awake, and the rude, thick corpse of her lover had yet to startle her heart. The big, communal house, inhabited by students, was beginning to stir. She heard running water, a clatter of pans from the kitchen. To keep the brutal dawn at bay, Gloria sucked her—no actually, her lover's—thumb as it lay clutched like a talisman in her small and unforgiving fist.